What people are saying about

The Silence Diaries

The quiet strength of *The Silence Diaries* is the way extraordinary people – a Fool, a political ventriloquist and a hearer of voices – are seen engaged in the everyday struggle for closeness and authenticity, a drama that resolves itself not in twists and denouements but in human virtues: patience, kindness and mutual understanding.
Philip Gross, winner of the T.S. Eliot Poetry Prize 2009, Wales Book of the Year 2010, National Poetry Competition

A sweet and gentle novel about how hard it can be to communicate honestly with others and be our real selves. In the frenzied, inauthentic world we have created, this is a book that reveals how the search for what is real and meaningful can sometimes be realised in unorthodox places: in the wisdom of fooling, the consolations of silence, not to mention the truculence of Bruce the ventriloquist's fox.
Paul Wilson, winner of the Portico Prize, author of *The Visiting Angel* etc.

The Silence Diaries

The Silence Diaries

Jennifer Kavanagh

Winchester, UK
Washington, USA

JOHN HUNT PUBLISHING

First published by Roundfire Books, 2019
Roundfire Books is an imprint of John Hunt Publishing Ltd., No. 3 East St., Alresford,
Hampshire SO24 9EE, UK
office@jhpbooks.com
www.johnhuntpublishing.com
www.roundfire-books.com

For distributor details and how to order please visit the 'Ordering' section on our website.

ISBN: 978 1 78904 182 8
978 1 78904 183 5 (ebook)
Library of Congress Control Number: 2018952029

A CIP catalogue record for this book is available from the British Library.

This is a work of fiction and not based on anyone alive or dead.

Design: Stuart Davies

UK: Printed and bound by CPI Group (UK) Ltd, Croydon, CR0 4YY
US: Printed and bound by Thomson-Shore, 7300 West Joy Road, Dexter, MI 48130

We operate a distinctive and ethical publishing philosophy in
all areas of our business, from our global network of authors to
production and worldwide distribution.

Hello, I'm Orbs, and occasionally Cyril.
I'm Suzie as well as Belinda.
I'm Freddie, and usually... Yes, yes, all right. Freddie.
And I'm Bruce.
Shut up, Bruce.

BRUCE AND BELINDA

Chapter 1

Tonight's the night. Even though I can't be there and she can't be here, I've done what I can to make it special.

I've fetched all the soft toys out of the store cupboard, and arranged them on the settee. In the old pine chest I found some tinsel, and wondered whether to blow up some balloons. I dug out the red piece of cloth that we throw over the settee when we want to look posh, and spread it carefully on the floor from the front door into the sitting room. I decided to keep the bubbly for later, but I took a beer out of the fridge and opened the packet of popcorn. I sat down among the animals and pressed the remote.

There she is. And him, of course.

Bruce and Belinda's Question Time. Of course, it's only a pilot, but everyone knows how much is hanging on it. It's a brilliant format. No questions in advance: a hard call for people who are used to interviews where prescripted questions enable them to prepare. And a sharper probing than is generally acceptable because it comes from a puppet and is sweetened by the charm of Belinda's interventions. Hard-soft, good cop – bad cop. B and B: Beauty and the Beast.

"So, Mr Mayor, how do you answer your critics?" Her sweetness of tone does not mask the directness of her questioning.

And then comes the probing snout, jeering. "Yes, Mr Mayor, Boris is right this time, isn't he?"

The "bad cop" is the puppet, Bruce, and the "good cop" is of course "Belinda", or Suzie, my Suzie.

It always takes me a while to get used to the blond wig and ridiculous makeup. It feels odd, too, watching it on my own, but as it's a live show, Suzie can hardly be with me, and I wasn't included in the specially invited audience because, in an attempt to harness the recent youthquake, they'd made the decision to invite only those aged between eighteen and twenty-five. Hard to accept that I'm past it!

I wonder how she's feeling. Nervous, I'm sure, but you'd never know it. She's always so self-contained. Whenever I see her on stage, she seems completely at home: her infectious smile embracing the audience. They love her, and she seems to know it. But this is different. Her own show. And live: there's nothing like live TV, they say, to get the adrenaline going.

For this show they've managed to get none other than Sadiq Khan. What a coup! Not actually Suzie's suggestion, though I know she's happy with it. It was always clear that, although Suzie would be consulted, the BBC would have the ultimate say. They've promised that if this pilot works, they'll consider commissioning a series. If they do, Suzie might get more say for future shows, as they begin to trust her. But for a kick-off she couldn't have asked for more.

Suzie Tavener is, of course, a respected financial journalist, and I'm Aubrey De'Ath Grimsby-Grenville (known as Orbs), a something in the City. That's how most people see us and how we often make our money.

Only, that's not who we are. In fact, Suzie is best known for something else entirely, and under another name. Suzie is a ventriloquist – or vent, as we call them – and her name is Belinda. But she keeps the two entirely separate. Never the twain shall meet. Actually, Suzie isn't well known at all. She's very much public property but very few people know who she is. Only a select few know her in either of her two worlds and hardly anyone other than me knows of the connection between them.

As for me, I also have a hidden life, and another name, but my life is even more secret, because I am not well known and Cyril isn't exactly a name to conjure with (so to speak!).

The first thing to say about me is that I'm not a clown. I'm not one of those sinister creatures hiding God knows what behind white faces and scaring the wits out of passers-by. No, I'm a fool. Silly name but with a proud history. Every culture has its tales about fools. The fool as truth-teller, the child-like person who sees through the stupidities and falseness of the age. Look at the wisdom of Shakespearean fools, see what power there is in the fool, what we have to offer the world. Yes, we wear a costume and a red nose, but being a fool isn't about hiding; for me, it's about presenting who I am, my true self, more truly myself than any of my more publicly acceptable personae. You could say that the difference between a clown and a fool is the difference between a maze, a place of confusion where you get lost, and a labyrinth, where there is only one way in, one centre, one truth. A place of trust. Finding, not losing, yourself.

Opinion is split about having a fool name. I have one, but I tend not to use it – it's not a separate part of myself, after all, but the essential part of me. The best part of me. You may have heard of Holy Fools – people like Roly Bain – well, I'm not a person of faith, but we do the same sorts of things. Some fools speak, but not in my tradition. We sometimes use our voices to make sounds, maybe sing, but not communicate in a traditional way by speaking. Shutting down one sense, I find, intensifies the others. I listen, hear and see much more keenly. Of course I'm not silent in my daily life. When Bruce allows us to get a word in, Suzie and I chat about everything under the sun.

I realise I haven't introduced Bruce. Remiss of me. Bruce is a fox with long and deceptively soft fur shading from cream to brown. But there's nothing cutesy or naff about him. Basil Brush he's not. Bruce is a much tougher affair, with a far from amiable expression and a hard snout for sniffing out the truth. Though it pains me to say so, he's rather magnificent.

Looking back at the screen, I can see that Suzie is in her element. From the first moment of this programme it's been clear that she has the knack of drawing out the truth from her victims. With all his intelligence and political experience, Sadiq is charmed. So by the time B&B home in on some of his key policies and question the discrepancy between rhetoric and action, they have him on the ropes.

Charm and intelligence: it's an unbeatable combo, a perfect expression of my girl's political instincts. Because Suzie has a politics degree, she's bright. She's also a couple of years older than me, which gives me an excuse for her greater success. She started on a political weekly and eventually was invited to do a monthly column of her own for both the print and the online versions. Like everything she does, it's original. It's a gossip column, not from within Westminster, but from the people on the street. She's always been good at engaging with Joe and Betty Bloggs, and feels strongly that it's their views that need to be heard. So her column is Vox Pop. And because it's not about her, it's anonymous.

Until her performance career took off, journalism was how Suzie made a living and it's always a fall-back position. Not that it looks as if that will be needed anytime soon, or ever if things carry on like this. But she's kept up her column, kept her skills and contacts ticking over. And in any case, her knowledge of grassroots opinion feeds into what she is doing on the show, providing her own oblique and unique contribution to political discourse.

The idea for the series came from the political editor of BBC TV who was in Edinburgh on holiday, and happened to pop in to her act. When he saw her coming out after the show he was gob-smacked to discover that the blond-headed "Belinda" was, in fact, the Suzie that he'd bumped into at political parties.

"I thought you looked familiar, but I would never have imagined it was you. Never in a month of Sundays." Amazing how seeing someone in a different context throws the mechanics of our memories. That was Suzie's protection.

Geoff was captivated and soon realised the potential of what he'd seen. Suzie's performing skills combined with her political nous: the astringent sharpness so evident from her columns together with the sweet demeanour of her stage presence made a winning combination. And it was then that he had his brainwave. *Why not*, he thought, *have a new form of political interview?* The following morning, he invited Suzie for a walk along Portobello beach and, as he walked, he outlined his idea.

"Political satire is nothing new, of course," he said, "but so many comedians don't go beyond the usual easy targets. This could combine the satire of *Dead Ringers* or *Spitting Image* with the straightforward interview of public figures. A double-pronged attack. No one's done anything like it."

It was quite a lot to take in, but Geoff was persuasive. "You've got the skill. You've got the political background. You could do it, Suzie." And squeezed her arm.

Suzie stopped and stood for a while, watching the waves. She could feel her excitement rising. *Yes*, she thought, *I could. No script for me, no preparation for them.* This could work.

"Okay," she said. "You're on. But one condition: you must keep stumm. Not a word." God knows why Suzie has this thing about secrecy, but that's part of who she is.

Watching the show, I'm so proud of her. I'm falling in love with her all over again.

I first fell for her over the footlights just over two years ago, dazzled by the extraordinary talent of this girl, her charm and audience skills so different from the rather sad (usually male) nerds who retreat into the personae of their puppets. I know some people think ventriloquism is creepy, but there's nothing creepy about my gal. I couldn't believe that she was unattached. How could that be? In the early days of our relationship, during those embarrassing exploratory conversations, Suzie wasn't very forthcoming. Dismissively, she said that none of her previous relationships had been serious. Saying what I wanted to hear, I guess. But perhaps I was never confident enough to believe her.

How was it that a lovely girl like her had ended up with me? When Suzie brought Bruce on our first date, I was amused, charmed even, but I have to say that in bed the charm wore thin. For Bruce is always there. Although Suzie doesn't usually throw her voice at home, unless she's practising for her show, and that she does mostly in the privacy of the bedroom, Bruce is a constant companion, a seeming attachment in almost every waking moment. When we're watching TV, he is usually on her arm, nodding, inclining his head back and forth, expressing his non-vocal opinions, and hiding from the scary bits with his head under his wing or on Suzie's shoulder. I've tried remonstrating with her, but I guess she can't help it. Goes with the territory. I've tried to be patient. I thought that as she got to know me it would wear off. Pathetic, I know, but after a while her divided attention began to make me feel insecure, like a reflection on my manhood, questioning my devastating attraction as a lover.

Not that I'm much of a catch. Fairly ordinary looking, wiry if you're being polite, scrawny if I'm honest, with big ears, and financially in a permanent state of wobble. My parents still think I'm some sort of Hooray Henry in the City, a world alien enough to them for me to keep up the façade, especially as I don't see much of them. Whereas for me London has been a liberation, they hate it, and rarely visit. In fact, I do some filling in at the bank from time to time to earn a few much-needed pennies – but at a lowly level in the accounts department, nothing flashy. Lucky to get in, actually, especially with such a flexible arrangement, but contacts and all that, who you know. Mum and Dad have no idea of what I actually do.

My other life started about seven years ago when, on a whim, I joined an evening class at the Circus Space. I just had to have some light relief from the tedium of office life. At first it was just a way of having fun and then I found it was much more than that. I absolutely loved it – not the juggling, high wire acts and so on, but the clowning. Such fun. It didn't occur to me as a job: I was too much my father's son. But after a couple of years of sheer boredom – and, yes, misery – the only thing I could think of that had given me joy were those two terms of evening classes. So I looked around and began to dream.

Even in our business it's who you know, so I contacted our clown teacher, Joe. He was doing a couple of gigs at Greenbelt and invited me along, expenses paid, to be his "glamorous assistant". I managed to fend off his advances, and had a really good time. It was so good to spark off an audience. After that, Joe persuaded me to do a residential workshop on the subtle art of fooling and, although I could barely afford it, I went. And discovered that it was not a possible job but a way of life. A way of being that expressed my self more profoundly than any other kind of social exchange. It was a transformation. For the first time in my life I knew what it was to feel at ease.

When I got into show biz, I realised how limited my all-male existence had been – family, school, and the City: that too was pretty male-dominated. Because when I encountered girls, women, however tongue-tied I was to begin with, I realised how much I liked this different species. Why had it taken me so long? They were definitely preferable. But I started late, so even by the time I met Suzie at twenty-eight, I wasn't very experienced.

Suzie and I "get" each other; we live in the same world and don't need to spell it all out. After all that dreary soul-searching that my previous girlfriend went in for – analysing our emotions all the time – it's such a relief. Though I know my fooling training is about emotional honesty, as a continual practice it's all a bit exhausting.

That isn't the only difference between the two women. Eva, my ex, was bipolar and somewhat unpredictable, which in the end was more than I could bear. Suze, on the other hand, is always her sunny, joyful self. Maybe it helps to transfer her negativity to a puppet. Bruce is a grumpy old thing, the Victor Meldrew of the puppet world, Meldrew with a Yorkshire accent

– maybe Boycott is nearer the mark. Yes, he sounds like Geoffrey Boycott.

Suzie doesn't like me criticising him. Once, when I called him grumpy, she turned on me. "He's not the only one. You have a grumpy voice too. I know, I've heard you." Too true. It's usually silent but sometimes I find that I've said something under my breath, and someone's heard it and is shocked. And what I had to say about that dratted puppet was mostly unrepeatable.

It's amazing that Suze can apparently change her personality so completely and, with her bright clear tones, can throw her voice into such a gruff *basso profundo*. I can't imagine that it can be good for the vocal chords, but Suze says there's no strain, it's no problem.

When we met, I was living an itinerant life – moving all over the country from one festival or gig to another. Not so much abroad – I couldn't afford it – but London, Edinburgh, Brighton, Leeds and a few smaller events. I wasn't living anywhere. Or rather, as the Scots say, wasn't staying anywhere. Of course I was living! Scraping a living, perhaps, travelling the circuit, cadging a night on a sofa in the flat of anyone who would have me. Friends were good – we are all pretty used to the struggles of the entertainment world. And smartphones have made it all possible. They also enable me to take calls from my parents without them needing to know where I am (or where I'm not). Suzie had just taken on this place in Bow, and was wondering if she could afford it on her own. So it made sense for me to move in.

I don't think I'm too much trouble. I'm used to living in other people's spaces, adapting to their ways, and the rhythms of their lives. I do my bit; I'm pretty domesticated, really. In my previous life I got to know who needed the shower when, what time it was civilised to appear in the morning or disappear at night, which way to hang the loo paper or the mugs on the hooks on the wall. And in that world no one is coy – we're always moving about the bathroom or changing room in various stages of undress. This is a small flat but big enough for the two of us, especially as we're both away so much. And it's really convenient. Near the DLR and only about half an hour into town – less than that by bike. And at the same time it has a distinct character of its own. Mainly Bangladeshi, but with some older original East Enders and a few newer incomers from Somalia and Eastern Europe. People are friendly when you get to know them, and living above a shop as we do, we are in close proximity to our neighbours, both below and on either side. We are set back from the main road so aren't generally bothered by the sound of the traffic. It's amazing how quiet it can be.

Although Suzie is far more sociable than I am, strangely, since I moved in with her, I've seen fewer people. Whereas in my sofa-surfing days it was hard to get away from people, most of Suzie's socialising goes on away from the flat or when I'm away. I'm sure her friends are very nice but, to be frank, I'm glad of the chance to have my own space.

* * *

After the programme, I put some bubbly in the fridge and fell asleep on the settee. Suzie came in in the early hours, looking tired but happy. I scrambled to my feet and held out my arms. She looked down at the cloth on the floor.

"What's that doing there?"

"Red carpet. Best I could do."

She then raised her eyes and saw the settee and its adornments. She giggled, leaned into my open arms, and said, "Oh, Orbs, you are silly!" I hugged her to me, but somehow got tangled up in her coat.

"Don't, you'll squash Bruce."

I said, "To hell with Bruce," and hugged her anyway.

Suzie was too tired to drink the bubbly and I was happy

enough to go to bed. Even when tired she is usually persuadable. As she curled up in my arms, she asked sleepily, "We were okay, weren't we?"

Indeed. Magnificent. A star is born.

I shouldn't have been surprised. Even when we'd first met, when Suzie was new to the game, you could see that she was going places. From the beginning, she glowed with the confidence of success. At Edinburgh she played to full houses; her reputation had preceded her. She wasn't eligible for the Comedy award, as what she does, though sometimes funny, isn't strictly speaking comedy, but her award for emerging artist brought her to the attention of the media, and, more to the point, the producers. Her agent was kept busy. I know I'm biased, but it's not just me that thinks she's an exceptional talent. I know, because Suzie has told me, that a vent performance works not just because of technical ability, but because of the material. No point in doing it if you can't engage the audience. And Suzie engages as much by force of personality as by her skill. God, I do love her.

Suzie has always been into mimicry. Apparently, she used to entertain the other kids at school by imitating their teachers, especially the gruff voice of Miss Patterson, the games teacher. It got her into trouble once or twice, but made her popular with her classmates. Of course she'd have been popular anyway, but I guess some of them might have been jealous of such a lovely talented girl. Maybe the fooling about was a way of deflecting their attention from her burgeoning good looks.

I remember that first time when I came round to the flat. That tremulous time when we were sussing each other out, when I was fancying her rotten but finding it hard to believe she wanted me, or that I'd be up to it if she did. That moment when Suzie shyly opened the door to her bedroom, and I braced myself to make a move. Instead of which, she introduced me to the soft animals that lined her bed. Patience, Orbs.

Picking up a ragged little brown monkey, she said, "This is

Naughty. I've had him since I was about two. And this", picking up a slightly grubby white unicorn with a gold horn and an appealing grin, "this is Cloud, who you could say started it all. My aunt Sophie gave him to me for my tenth birthday. As Cloud's a bag" (she showed me the zip at the back) "I carried her around all the time, and even strangers in the street made comments, talked to me because of her. Everyone loved her, and I felt people liked me because of her. And then, later, I realised that people liked me even without her, and then, when I got other animals, puppets, it became more fun to make them the bad guys, so I would shine in comparison."

Suzie said that she'd never wanted proto-human dolls for her act. She was always more attracted to animals, like the soft toys that she used to talk to as a child. But in a home where visits from friends were not encouraged, she found that the one-way conversation was not enough; she wanted them to talk back. I'd known other girls who still had their childhood creatures round their bed. It was rather endearing, even when they talked to them like a favourite pet. But I'd never met one who talked through them. That gorgeous glorious girl seemed to have nothing to do with the grumpy old fox attached to the end of her left arm.

To begin with, Suzie told me, she got her puppets from charity shops, sometimes adjusting soft animals to have mobile jaws, for instance, to make them work as puppets. But recently she'd invested in a professionally made vent puppet. Time to get serious.

Of course, the TV show is not the same as Suzie's stage act, what she won her award for, which was mostly a debate between her and Bruce, but the creative nub came from her intervention with the audience. Her most recent Edinburgh show involved Bruce using a mobile phone – so it became a three-way conversation. I marvelled at her skill, and the audiences loved it.

But TV, that's quite a different matter. How would it be if it really took off? If she were really famous? If millions tuned in every week to see how the combined attack of B&B could winkle out the truth? TV will bring in a hefty sum, especially in the wake of that row about the gender gap at the BBC. It's bad enough feeling dependent on Suzie's income as it is; if she becomes really rich, and everyone sees me as a parasite, it could be our undoing.

When Suzie told me about the pilot, I was nervous. "But, Suzie, television. What about us?"

Her look was quizzical. "What about us?"

"Well, you'll get well known and recognised in the street. Our lives won't be our own any more."

Suzie laughed. "Don't be silly, Orbs. I have a different stage name, so no one will know. And anyway, we don't know that there will be a series and, round here, no one's likely to watch."

I don't know the watching habits of my largely Bangladeshi neighbours but perhaps that's true.

"Aren't you pleased for me?"

I squeezed her arm. "Of course I am, darling. I'm so proud of you. I just don't want things to change."

"Silly billy." Suzie kissed me reassuringly. But I knew things would change. Couldn't fail to. The grand life. New territory for Suzie. I hoped she wouldn't get too used to it – it wasn't something I wanted to join her in. I'd no wish to join in all that celebrity crap. But I could see the temptation, and I was afraid.

She was doing pretty well as it was. Landing a show on terrestrial TV is a huge breakthrough for any act regarded as "fringe", though you have only to see the success of the oldies like *Sesame Street* to see that puppets can take off. Though vent acts have been out of fashion for a while, they seem to be coming back. Her show was for adults, of course, which is quite different, and she's a woman. Though her hero Nina Conti has made a great success, it's mainly in one-off shows and after-dinner speaking, not a potential series like B&BQs. And this was political, which was unique.

* * *

It was almost immediately apparent that our hopes (and fears) had been realised. As soon as the show went live, it was trending on Twitter and the following morning the reviews were superb. Bruce and Belinda's question time (or B&BQs, as it has quickly become known) was a hit.

The morning after, unsurprisingly, Suzie slept in, but even as she slept, her voice mail and in-box were filling up. With congratulations from friends, and messages from others who wanted to get in on the act – "Suzie, have you thought of...?" Messages from people she barely remembered. "Hi, Suzie, we haven't met up for ages. How about...?" All pretty commonplace in her world, but up the scale this time – indeed, almost off the scale. In self-defence, Suzie kept off social media, letting her agent do the needful.

After a sketchy kind of leftovers brunch we flopped on the settee with our coffees, a bit lacklustre after all the excitement.

"Is Jessie pleased?" Her agent is always on the ball. Tweeting all over the place.

"Thrilled to bits. She says I've got over a thousand new followers. Whatever that means." We're neither of us social media types. Can't be bothered. Haven't got the time.

"A-maz-ing. Good for you."

At the weekend we wandered round our city like tourists, picnicking in Kew Gardens, taking the slow boat to Greenwich. Holding hands, ordinary people, ordinary life. Stopping the world and getting off, just for a little, and maybe for the last time. Whole days without Bruce. Suzie didn't wear him when she was out in public – it would blow her cover – but I knew he was there in her bag.

Chapter 2

It took a while for things to calm down. And then we entered into a strange period of suspension where everything was normal on the outside but underneath was seething with expectation. It wasn't so much the decision: we didn't have to wait long for that. Within a few weeks, the producer, Emily, was on the phone to check that Suzie had kept the relevant autumn dates free. Assuming the best, she had already checked out the availability and willingness of some possible victims. And the following week Emily confirmed that the series had been given the green light to run in September. Not at prime time, as Suzie had hoped, but a later evening slot on Tuesdays on BBC 2. Suzie was disappointed, but knew too that if it had been on BBC 1 and earlier, she would have had no chance of keeping the press off her back. As it was, we might just escape.

But then we had long months of being forbidden to speak of it. No leaks until the publicity was ready to go. Which suited me. I've got used to keeping things quiet and there were few people I could have shared it with anyway. I have no wish for media mayhem at any time and if it had to happen, the later the better. I knew it was inevitable, and dreaded the news breaking. I could just imagine it:

Vent Queen Breaks into TV

Move over Paxo! B&BQs is on its way

After the pilot, the plaudits poured in and so did the scarcely veiled sexual invitations.

Suzie laughed them off, paid them little attention, but on advice from Jessie we took measures to improve our security, both online and in the flat. What a drag it all was. It almost made me hanker after my more nomadic way of life. It felt as if Suzie's success was already taking its toll, of her – and of me. Putting up with my partner being public property, subject to sexual innuendo from any Tom, Dick or Harry. I had every reason to be jealous. But it wasn't infidelity or the attention of other men that I feared. There was only one creature who absorbed Suzie's attention, and that was Bruce. Silly, isn't it? Pathetic.

In the meantime Suzie was immensely busy in preparation, on the phone night and day, and in seemingly end-to-end meetings and lunches with producer and agent. It was natural for her to be tense, excited, preoccupied. Natural, I told myself, that she should be more caught up with Bruce. But I couldn't help feeling shut out, resentful. It didn't help that I'd taken a leave of absence from the bank. It's boring work, but a diversion, all the same. At home I tried to keep things as normal as possible, taking on more of the household chores than usual and seeking to distract her, but the tension was palpable.

When Suzie emerged late one evening from a practice session with her puppet, hair tousled, looking, I thought, a bit ragged, I patted the settee next to me, and put an arm round her. She was resistant, fidgety, her mind elsewhere.

"Bath?"

"Oh, I don't know..."

"Oh, come on, Suze, you've got to relax sometime. Let go for a bit."

One of our few routines is that on the nights when we're both in, we try to share a bath with some of Suzie's smellies – "aromatherapy, darling; it'll help you relax" – and some of my little yellow plastic ducks. Maybe some candles round the side, and certainly a glass of wine. We sit facing each other, and playing with each other's toes. It's a time for a giggle, a time to wind down, talk through the day and, if we're lucky, it can be a prelude to more expansive fun in bed. But now, it had all got so serious that we rarely found the time.

So on this evening I was determined to make the most of it. Once the bath was deep and warm enough, we climbed into our old-fashioned high-sided tub. I leaned back against the taps, gazing at her unblemished loveliness: her creamy skin, the tawny tuft between her legs softened by the water, and wondered how I could be so lucky. And when she turned for me to soap her back I was treated to the sight of the delicious little seahorse tattoo at the base of her spine. I'm not sure that my front or back provided such an alluring vista.

But we stayed and soaked and sank into the warmth, eventually emerging in a glow of heat, and barely bothering to rub each other dry before tumbling into bed.

* * *

As the summer wore on, we braced ourselves for the inevitable media invasion. Our only hope was that the start of the series would coincide with the revelation of the new *Strictly* celebrities. We just had to hope that the media would be diverted, and that the Beeb would honour the terms of the contract, because Suzie's agreement to do the show came with one condition. There was to be no connection made between her life as a journalist and her life as a vent, between Vox Pop and Belinda. Her identity had to be kept secret. Her agent too was on notice: any leaks, and she'd be out. Suzie could be tough where her professional life was concerned.

I didn't altogether understand her fierce need for anonymity in almost all realms of her life. I could see that Vox Pop needed to be anonymous – it was the voice of the people, after all. But her identity as a vent?

"Orbs," she would say. "I'm a journalist. If Belinda creeps out of the woodwork, bang goes my credibility."

During this time, it helped that for a couple of weeks I was on cat duty – a pleasant nightly diversion just before our own suppertime. When I was a kid, my parents had a long-haired cat, and as an adult I missed being able to cosset what I call (but never in Suzie's hearing) a real animal. With our peripatetic way of life there's no way we could have one ourselves, so it's nice to have the opportunity to be around a live animal again. Palash and Hannah and their kids live above the fruiterers next door but one, and we got to know each other a little when we both complained about the night-time noise from the office between us. When they're away I'm always happy – never so much as now – to pop in and feed their delightful little Manisha.

I let myself in and dismantled the alarm, with Manisha winding round my ankles.

"Come on, you. Anyone would think you hadn't eaten for a week."

I took my time, wandering round the flat as she scoffed what was on her plate. It's a bigger flat than ours, with two proper bedrooms and an extra living room, but I imagine it's still a bit cramped with two children, and will be even more difficult as they get older. I spent longer in the kids' room, fingering the toys: brightly coloured tops, wooden building blocks, a doll's house, and some soft animals – but I've seen enough of those! I then sat with Manisha on my lap, stroking her, and soaking up the vibrations of her purr. She's a large cat, ginger and white, which is apparently rare for a female. I don't know much about cats, but have always enjoyed their independence and sleek sensuousness. A real animal. As I sat there for a few minutes every evening, enjoying the warmth of her on my knees and the silky feel of her fur, I was struck more than ever by the oddity of our lives with Bruce. How had I come to accept it?

Chapter 3

Although what we do is in different spheres, Suzie and I both work without a script – for both of us that's something fundamental to the creative process. I wonder how Suzie's interviewees are going to cope with that – it'll be a hard act for people who are used to having the questions in advance. Tough. Because in this instance Suzie can call the shots. Though she knows never to ask questions to which she doesn't know the answer!

It's great that Suze and I are, well almost, in the same line of business, because it means we can spend more time together, on the road. We lead a nomadic life, here and there, sometimes together, sometimes alone. It keeps us fresh, it's what makes it all work. Suzie travels quite a lot for her column anyway, so she sometimes manages to combine it with a gig. If she's researching a column on, say, education, there's no reason why she shouldn't be chatting to mothers outside school gates in a town that happens to have a festival, in Brighton, Manchester or wherever. She doesn't record them, doesn't identify them. Doesn't wander about with a mic. She simply wants to listen, relying on her own impressions, her own memory. She just has a gift for getting people to talk to her. A bunch of women in a fish queue, men signing on, or people sitting in a hospital waiting room. She just takes the temperature of the nation in an unattributable way. And when people read her column in the paper or online, they know it's real.

We don't do all the same gigs. Suzie's work isn't comedy, really, so she fits better into the broader-based festivals. But it's great when we can go together. Though she's usually the main act, on the stage, and I'm a side show in a tent somewhere in a boggy field. But that's cool. Fooling isn't about success. It's about failure, actually. And I'm fine with that. No, I am.

I learned right at the beginning how to deal with failure

without feeling rubbish. On our fools' course, we all performed for each other. There were usually about fifteen of us sitting on the floor in front of a stage. Two people with red noses on the stage. We are willing them to be funny, but if they aren't, they aren't. "Off!" shouts Joe, the teacher. "Get off." That was just for our spontaneous performances, but he also asked us to prepare a solo show to perform in front of the others. He warned us: "I'm going to fail you all," but we didn't really believe him and worked our socks off to make our performances as good as they could be. When in due course we were failed, it was okay. The sky didn't fall in. We didn't have to fear failure; we knew we could survive.

Fooling is about flow, about what Zen calls Beginner's Mind. Being in the present with no expectations, as if seeing everything for the first time. No plans, which is pretty scary. Sometimes, when I'm fooling on my own, I manage it, especially when wearing my nose. Though sometimes it seems that others see my being present as vacuous. Foolish, as in having little up top, permanently.

Generally speaking, fooling is my line, not Suzie's, but despite the seriousness of her journalism and even of her vent shows, she has her playful side, and I love it when she lets her fool emerge.

Take last October. We both had a clear day, so decided to do some fooling together. To go on the tube in costume, and see what happened. Suzie had to do a good deal of scrabbling around the evening before to find some appropriate clothes.

From her kneeling position on the floor in front of a pile of discarded clothes, she looked up at me and said in her best cut glass: "Dahling, I've got simply *nothing* to wear!"

So, we got up at about midday – had to avoid the rush hour – and dressed as usual in silence, taking serious care with each piece of clothing. Then we stood and looked at each other. I couldn't be serious when I saw Suzie in her silly little net tutu and sparkly tights, and hoped that others would feel the same.

"Circle Line?"

"Yeah, that way we can just go round and get off when we want." Suzie slung a big pink love-heart-covered bag over her arm and we went out of our front door, down the steps and into the street. On show.

At Liverpool Street, Suzie hissed in my ear, "Which way?"

"Doesn't matter."

And then we were silent. With people staring (and pretending not to notice), we went down the escalator and got on the tube.

For a while we just sat there opposite each other, smiling at our neighbours and letting them take us in. Then Suzie reached into her bag, and pulled out a red and a yellow balloon. With exaggerated huffing and puffing, we blew them up and began to bat them to each other back and forth. We had such fun. The highlight was an encounter with a small boy on crutches, and his delight as we batted a balloon to him and he used it to hit his carer over the head.

In general people were wary – we're used to that and are careful not to intrude on anyone who obviously doesn't want to know. People stared at us from a safe distance: from the platform, from the next carriage, but only occasionally had the courage to engage directly with us. We're a reserved lot, we Brits, and having learned to overcome my own inhibition, I now try to encourage others to conquer theirs. It's such a liberation. But I must say that the selfie culture has really brought people out of themselves. It seems much more normal now to want photos of silly things, including ourselves.

It's fun, too, getting people laughing, kids, even in hospital. Some of my friends work with refugees and old people with dementia. I prefer just to get out in the streets and see what comes up, connecting with people – lightening up their life. I remember a woman bus driver stuck in traffic. When I waved, she waved back, and we did it again until I got into a frenzy of waving, jumping up and down, and she was in stitches. Hope it made her day.

Coming from the family that I do means that overcoming the hurdle of engaging with strangers has been scary. People like us don't do that sort of thing. But as fools we only engage with people when they want to – and often they do, seeing our silliness for what it is – a bit of playfulness to punctuate the day. And it gives them permission. Sometimes nothing happens. And that's fine, too. I know I keep saying that's fine. But it is. As long as you stay with it. More fine anyway than having to behave like that upper-class twit I was brought up to be. More real, more me. And sometimes I get a gig, earn some money. There's nothing like feeling an audience with me, whether laughing or emotionally stirred. It can go either way.

Sometimes it will only work if I'm in costume. For instance, when I'm waiting at a bus stop, I can't imagine how people would respond if I suddenly started waving in a silly manic way at passing cars. Or at that bus driver. Costume is like a uniform: it authenticates our behaviour for others and we believe in it more ourselves. And, because it's so noticeable, it's also a statement. When I joined the jollity of a local street party, and went to sit next to a solitary man, it would have meant nothing if I hadn't been in costume. It would have been just two lonely old gaffers sitting on a bench. As it was, it showed solidarity.

Paid work is hard to come by. Even as a straight actor it's a precarious life – flitting from one small theatre to another, trundling round the country and abroad – am actor, will travel. It's a restless way of life, the only certainty the boards beneath your feet. And, as for the rarefied world of fooling, it's even harder – no parts, no auditions. Any opportunities come mostly by word of mouth. Festivals are fruitful – rarely so full that they can't open up a chink and allow in another act. But, mostly, you just have to make your own way – create your own path. Ideas plus self-promotion, something I'm not very good at. A couple of years ago, just before I met Suzie, in a burst of energy and taking care to steer clear of anything in my parents' neck of the woods, I hired myself out as a living scarecrow.

As well as keeping the birds away, the scarecrow was a publicity stunt for the farmers, advertising their shops and "pick your own". For me, the reward was board and lodging, some good fresh air and welcome solitude, and a small fee for my trouble. "Paid work" is a pretty flexible term. My scarecrow gigs were something to put on the CV, but it was pretty shattering work. I'm an active bloke, so after a couple of hours my legs and back began to complain. How those mostly unmoving statues do it, I can't imagine. I had to negotiate frequent breaks, and even then, after a couple of two-week gigs, I gave it up. Not wanting to waste the costume, I took the scarecrow to some festivals and found some fields to stand in. There were a lot of selfies and a few coins in the hat.

Chapter 4

This is a great place to live. Occasionally, I compare it a bit wistfully with the high ceilings and large rooms of my previous digs, in a spacious Victorian flat in Camden, but then I remember how cold and draughty it was in winter. Our little flat can be a bit stuffy, but at least it's warm.

And there's plenty of green space. Mile End Park is quite near, but just round the corner is the cemetery. It's also a park, actually, a nature reserve in fact, and hasn't been used for burying people for years. Suzie can't stand the place – says it gives her the creeps – but I find it soothing to wander among the dilapidated graves. The angels, monuments, crosses, and stones of all heights and sizes, many leaning drunkenly together. "Dearly beloved", "Ebenezer", "fell asleep". Delightfully old-fashioned. It does no harm to think of our mortality from time to time. Though I suppose I don't know anyone close who has died, except my grandparents and that was too long ago for me to remember. Dad's parents died in the war, so I never knew them anyway. So death doesn't touch me in the way it seems to touch others, including Suzie.

But, most importantly, near the railway, there's the labyrinth. It's misnamed the Chalk Maze, hidden among trees and long grass, and somewhat hard to find, especially in the summer, when it's almost completely overgrown and you can hardly see the chalk path for the grass. Last time I walked it, I revelled in a riot of flowers in yellow, purple and white – cow parsley, cowslip and clover – and a number I didn't recognise, and was accompanied by bees and the occasional cabbage white. No one seems to go there, so I generally have it to myself.

Walking a labyrinth means a lot to me. It affects me in a mysterious way. It calms me, places me in the present moment. In the middle I can ask for guidance, and sometimes feel clearer minded when I emerge, or later, when the process has worked its way through me. Although there is just one way in and the same way back, the journeys are not the same. The path may be the same, but the experience is different; I feel changed.

Labyrinths are very ancient. I can't remember when I first heard about them, but when I was in my teens I remember coming across one near my parents' farm, and finding it a good place to hide away from all the family stuff. It was large, octagonal not round, and I can still remember the scent of the rosemary bushes that served as markers at some of the corners. One of the things that I like about labyrinths is that just as you seem to be approaching the centre, you're actually furthest away, and when you seem to be at the edge you are actually heading to the centre. I don't know what that means but it feels significant. Although there are any number of designs, I think that's true of all of them. A few years ago, an artist put a little enamel labyrinth somewhere on a wall of every underground station in London. There are over 250 of them, each one different: some squat and chunky, some elongated, even flower-like. At one time I fantasised about finding them all, but I soon gave up. I'm not that methodical. But I do try to look out for them when I'm in a tube station and, sometimes, depending on how "out there" I want to be with my fooling, I ignore the curious looks of passers-by and trace one with my finger.

There's a labyrinth near work in that no-man's land between the Bank and Fenchurch Street station. It's startling to find one in the massive shadows of the Gherkin and all those looming towers, but there it is: a simple little pattern of brown gravel path and grey borders made up of small square stones, settled, defiantly making its space felt. It's extraordinary how the experience of walking in such a small place, overshadowed as it is, can bring such a sense of openness. The problem is that, as hardly anyone recognises what it is, people walk across the middle, sit on the benches round the outside and eat their sandwiches. When

I walk it, it's hard to concentrate and ignore the amused and critical gaze of other office workers. It's particularly hard to do it in a city suit. So I only go there when I'm feeling strong.

Living in London can be the best and worst of experiences. On the one hand, people plod along as if the world and shopping are weighing them down; they sit or stand in overcrowded tubes, squashed up against each other's armpits. It's a huge, anonymous and sometimes lonely place. You could die alone and it might be weeks before the smell alerted anyone. There would be no milkman to sound the alarm and the postman might always ring twice, but it would be a different one every time.

On the other hand, the very anonymity of the city allows for the zany to express itself. And that's what I love about it. Whereas in my parents' village, people know your every move, and probably disapprove, here people leave you alone and allow you to be. Look at the clothes. Who needs costume when you can wear what you like? Sundress or burka, long or short, skimpy or voluminous, plain or brilliantly exotic, T-shirt or full morning dress.

When you keep your eyes open, opportunities for play are everywhere. Just the daily dance along London streets. In costume, the impact on someone coming towards you, head in mobile phone, is a delight as they suddenly look up to be confronted by a smiling strangely dressed person who hasn't dodged out of the way. Then there's the young man in the next road to ours, cycling up and down on one wheel, the man I saw crossing the road, juggling, as he went, and another juggling oranges in a Soho shop doorway. The lone bagpiper on Hampstead Heath and the Algerian guy outside my bike shop, who has set up a coffee stall with flowers growing from a box he carries on the back of his bike. He says coffee grounds help the flowers grow, and offered some to me for my non-existent window box.

It's when I see people like that that I know I'm not alone.

There are other people who, without saying a word, seek to make the world a jollier place. No, not seek, because they seem to do it without trying. It's not just animals who are naturally playful.

There are so many playful opportunities in London; in fact, there is positive encouragement. There are free pianos at St Pancras station and Canary Wharf – all over the place; ping-pong tables in city squares, even in the patio at the BBC. People are becoming less averse to letting their hair down. Flash mobs, you name it. The selfie culture has changed everything, turning what used to be a spectator sport into becoming part of the spectacle. It's all right to be silly if you can film yourself doing it. Of course, that's a delight for anyone whose life centres round play. The more fun, the better.

And for the pros, at all the major tourist attractions – Trafalgar Square, Covent Garden, the South Bank – there are street entertainers of every kind, from moving statues, jugglers, musicians, escapologists to the occasional fire eater. Some of the prime sites demand a performing licence, or a busking audition. Although it can be a bit restricting, I'm all for it really: can't be doing with having my eardrums assaulted by people who think they can sing or play. And there are still plenty of places where you can stop and play the fool, and even make some money. My top hat is sometimes quite heavy at the end of an afternoon.

But the confusion of amateur and professional does make it hard for those of us who are trying to make a living. The trouble is that the streets are crowded with people touting for money. The chuggers for this or that charity, Big Issue sellers, and others begging for the last quid or two to see them into a hostel. How can I compete – and should I? When I see a music student trying to supplement their income, I feel bad at getting in the way, even more by the sight and sound of an old guy on the street corner playing the accordion. Now there is someone who really needs bread – in both senses. For me to play alongside him is like taking it from him. And I can't even collect for charity, because then you do need permission.

Chapter 5

I heard Suzie stomping up the stairs. She flung in the front door, and slammed her bag down on the table. I wondered what was up. Suzie had been for a girls' night out, and I hadn't expected her back so soon.

"You're early, sweetie."

"It's begun."

I was nonplussed. "What has?"

"Andrea recognised me on the box."

"Oh. Oh, dear."

"She promised to keep it to herself, but—" Suzie shook her head. I could see she was trying not to cry.

I tried to console her but, to be frank, I wasn't surprised. I know that she had hoped that seeing her out of context and with a different name would put people off the scent. But her friends? Even with a wig, how could she think that they wouldn't spot her? What would be a bigger deal was if her journo friends made the connection. You could hardly expect them to keep it to themselves – they are newshounds after all. How on earth did Suzie imagine she could go on telly and remain private? It was tempting to say, "I told you so."

As long as they didn't track her down here. That was my greatest fear. How many people knew where we lived?

Suzie had to put her worries out of her mind. She had a lot on her plate, trying to get some of the research for her Vox Pop column under her belt before B&BQs took up all her time. When she wasn't out and about interviewing the great British public, she was rehearsing in front of the mirror at home. She showed little overt tension, but I noticed that she was clinging even more to Bruce. I even heard them arguing. She was in the bedroom at the time, so I had no idea what was going on. I was under strict orders never to interrupt her practice so it could have been part of her new show, but I had an uneasy feeling that it was "for real". That she was arguing with a puppet.

The waiting was getting to both of us. I felt tense, and more irritable than usual with the peculiar circumstances of our lives.

* * *

"Put that bloody thing away."

Suzie rolled over and put it on the bedside table. "Don't call him a thing." But she said it wearily, without passion. It was a scene that had been played out many times before. And not one that encouraged a romantic conclusion.

Unusually, Suzie fell asleep before me. I lay on my side looking down on my love, her dark hair spread across the pillow. And then looked beyond her to the heap of inert material lying on the bedside table, and wished it elsewhere, anywhere but here. I often fantasised about getting rid of him. But knew I'd then have to deal with the heartbreak that would follow and, even if I sometimes thought it might be better for Suzie not to be so dependent, I couldn't bring myself to do it. Other puppeteers have several puppets, do not have them with them all the time. For Suzie it was always Bruce. By the time we met, she'd been working with him for five years. He was an appendage – not only on her arm but in her heart. It really wasn't healthy. But she'd probably only get another one anyway. I had to face it, I was stuck with him. Jealous. I knew I was. I hated how he had to be babied, hushed, rested and settled for the night like a baby would be. At least Bruce didn't wake us in the night. Small mercies. But by the time Suze had gone through his bedtime routine, I was usually past any amorous inclination.

As a result, we made love less often. Our sex life, once so all-encompassingly wondrous, as I marvelled at so glorious a creature joining her body to mine, had gone into the doldrums. They say it's hard to keep up the momentum after the first six months, but it wasn't the dullness of habit that had defeated us. Suze's late nights and my early ones at the bank made it difficult to find time for leisurely exploration of each other. But, most of all, bloody Bruce was always in the back of my mind. I was beginning to feel more assertive about my place in her life. There weren't that many men who would put up with Bruce. Maybe it was true that none of her previous relationships had lasted. I'd been pretty tolerant, after all. But it was wearing thin.

To distract myself, I entered into a period of hyperactivity. I surprised Suzie by washing the floor, stocking up on supermarket goodies and making longer visits to the market. I also tried to spend some time getting back into my body. I tried to remember the exercises we'd been taught, and made an effort to set some time aside every evening to increase awareness of every part of my body – wriggling my toes, stretching my arms. To have a sense of how I feel in any given moment: a slight cramp in my left calf, relax the tension in my belly, unclench my hands, loosen my jaw. I'd also fallen out of the habit of regular exercise, so I tried to revive a regime of morning exercises: stretching, flexing, push-ups, squats. Just fifteen minutes or so. It made me feel better, but wasn't enough. Actors, and especially fools, have to be fit. All that falling, climbing, jumping – you never know what you might end up doing.

But I wasn't sure a gym was the answer. Although there's one not far away in Mile End, interacting with machines doesn't turn me on – and they're so damn expensive anyway. I must also confess that I don't feel very embedded in this part of London – we haven't really joined anything local. I flicked through the local rag which had just come through the letter box, and saw there was quite a lot going on. Jive classes? Or perhaps I should really push the boat out and sign up for a "total-body exercise class" called SwingTrain, which apparently happens here in Bow. A "high-intensity dance cardio workout" inspired by almost every retro dance you can think of, from Charleston to

Hot Jazz. Kill or cure.

I played safe, and decided instead to renew my membership of the outdoor swimming pool in town. I'd signed up when I lived in Camden, and loved the feel of swimming in the fresh air in the middle of a city: the sight of sunflowers in the summer and in the winter the steam rising from the water in the cool air. It's a bit of a trek on my bike but worth the effort.

I time my visits carefully, going late enough to avoid the speed merchants who pound up and down and splash a lot, and before the arrival of school or family contingents. Just after 9:00 a.m., there are just a few indistinguishable silver-headed biddies placidly breast-stroking their way up and down the slow lane, chatting with each other and the lifeguard. On this occasion there were still enough hefty blokes left in the changing room to make me feel inadequate. A reminder of all those schoolboy comparisons of size. I pulled on my trunks, pulled in my stomach and told myself not to be a prick.

The slow lane gives me more freedom to do what I want. Today, I decided to swim as slowly as I could without sinking, doing a little dog-paddle, indeed, transforming myself into a scruffy little terrier. Going swimming always brings out the child in me so I amused myself by dropping some toys I'd brought with me to the bottom of the deep end and diving down to get them. "Fetch!"

When I came up, I realised it was raining and as I swam towards the shallow end I started singing under my breath. "I'm swimming in the rain, just swimming in the rain."

Another man came up behind me. "She died, didn't she?"

"Sorry? Who?" Chatty lot, these swimmers.

"Debbie Reynolds."

Oh yes, I'd forgotten she'd been in it. It was just Gene Kelly that stuck in my mind. And Ore doing it on *Strictly*.

I'm always surprised how many fat people go swimming – I mean that they swim and remain fat – women with bulging upper arms, men with pot bellies. Fat but fit, I guess. Anyway, that's not my problem. I've convinced myself that it will help to keep me trim. And I enjoy it.

* * *

People-watching is very much part of the job. All the silliness of human behaviour – all those hand gestures when you're on the phone and the person on the other end can't see; the different way women walk when they're in flatties or in heels; glancing in every shop window that you pass to mirror your perfection (or insecurity); the authority vested in a weedy young man by a safety helmet, hi-vis jacket, large gloves and a purposeful look. It's all grist to the mill. People are endlessly fascinating and a great source of material for any performer. Of course, I don't mean I absorb their behaviour consciously – we don't plan – but it's added to the rich mix of memory. The public are both my material and my audience. There's no divide. Suzie and I are the opposite in that. For her it's all about performance, which she keeps quite separate from her daily existence. For me, it's all one.

Strange that we are both in fields that are particularly geared to children, but neither of us works with kids. In fact, neither of us has ever had much to do with them. Not that I'm averse to having some of my own one day, but that's beside the point. Although I have friends who make a living from performing at children's parties, it's not really my thing. What I do is not about prepared tricks, though I suppose if we needed to, it might be a way of making a bit of extra cash.

Having said that, when I stayed with a family with small children and assumed I might have to do some party tricks to earn my keep, it wasn't like that at all. I found that the kids were much more on my wavelength than the parents. We just hung out together and had fun. And they taught me a lot. Never perform, they say, with a child or an animal. They're better at it, that's why. Born show stealers.

Chapter 6

In the end no amount of distraction seemed to do the trick. Suzie was still completely preoccupied, so I thought it best to get myself out of the way. As I sat on the train, gazing out of grimy windows at the recently shorn golden fields, I let go of some of the urban stress and felt my body relax. It was good to get out of London and stretch my legs. I hoped I might stretch my mind too, get a better sense of direction.

Joe met me at the station. A quiet country station, with a one-way track, where you have to wait for the up train to pass before the signals change and the down train can come along. Joe lives in the middle of nowhere and he drove me off to that nowhere – a tumble-down cottage – for a sandwich lunch. By mutual consent we deferred any talk of serious matters until we were out on the fells.

I sat in the kitchen while Joe heated up a carton of soup and put a slab of cheese, a board and a loaf on the table. He put a steaming bowl in front of me, and sat down in front of his own.

I dipped in my spoon. "Don't you feel lonely, out here on your own?"

Joe considered. "That's two questions," he said. "Out here, not at all. I love the view of the hills, with nothing in the way, love the fact that no one bothers me. But, on my own, yes, sometimes. I miss having someone in my life, in my bed, miss having someone to talk it through with at the end of the day. But, then, if someone else was here, all this" – and he waved his arms around – "just wouldn't be the same." He grinned at the impossibility of it all.

Yes, I knew what he meant. I missed all that when Suzie was away. A life without Suzie would be seriously diminished, but I knew that my moments of deep stillness were always on my own.

Although I couldn't wait to get away from my parental home and London has proved my salvation, I have to admit that it was a delight to be out, to see the wide horizon, the big sky, smell the air and breathe again. I wouldn't like to live at the back of beyond, but I do crave wilderness from time to time. Maybe when the reminders of parental constraint have faded, but not just yet. Though it's certainly given a city-bred man like Joe a dollop of peace.

Joe is a short, prematurely balding Liverpudlian in early middle age, with a rubbery face that is ideal for the fooling game. He's one of the few people with whom I can be completely honest – indeed, I have no choice. You can't do a workshop with Joe without him demanding complete openness. It's not always an easy place to be.

"So," he said, as we set out, "how's it going?"

"No, you first. I want to hear how your latest show went."

"Glasgow? Oh, we stormed the place. We had a nice crowd, and Ranjit and Clare were a pleasure to work with."

"She's not been around for long, has she?" I remembered meeting her – a thin waif of a girl – at some gathering of fools.

"No, but we really gelled. There's something about her that touches people."

Yes, I could see how that might be.

"And Ranjit you know."

Indeed. Ranjit and I had started at the same time and shared our uncertainties. He is the nearest to a soul-brother that I have. The trouble is that he moved to the Shetlands and we are rarely in the same part of the world. When I think of fooling, my fondest memories are of our double acts, that sense of intuition that makes us respond to each other even before a move is made. He is tough, butch, immensely funny.

"And I'm off to Barcelona next week. They've asked me to run a workshop. That should be fun. Always is, when language is an issue. Just as well we don't talk!"

We negotiated a stile and set off across a track, with cows safely in the distance. It was a bit on the boggy side, and I was glad of my walking boots. Like me, they don't get enough exercise.

Joe turned to me. "How about you?"

"Well, I've not been doing much, and I suppose that's why I wanted to talk to you. To get some pointers. I really miss it, but am not sure where to go next."

"No, Orbs, I didn't ask what you've been doing, but how you are."

Ah. Yes.

I considered. "Well, actually, it's much the same thing. It's because I'm doing so little fooling, stuff I really love, that I have to spend all that time at the bank, doing unreal stuff. And then I feel, well, distorted."

"Distorted, yes." Joe pondered as he stepped round a large cow pat. "Well, how would it be if you were not 'distorted'? Can you imagine it? Would it actually matter what you did? Fooling is what we are, Orbs. It's not something to be kept for special occasions."

I trudged on, head down, kicking at the turf. "I know. I just need the special occasions to get me back in the groove, to remind me."

"Well, don't beat yourself up about it. No one says it's easy."

When we got the top of the tor, we sat for a while and surveyed the landscape. Distant patches of rock, isolated sheep, a buzzard wheeling.

"What a great place to live, Joe. So quiet."

"Too quiet sometimes."

"Really?" I couldn't imagine such a thing.

"After a while it can seem a bit much. There are times when I hanker after the hum of distant traffic."

I shook my head in disbelief, and we sat for a while without speaking.

Joe got up. "Shall we move on?" We walked down to a stream at the bottom of the hill. Full of water, it was burbling busily by from a rocky cascade further upstream through a quiet patch to the stepping stones at our feet.

"Yes, we've had a lot of rain."

Picking up a stick, Joe threw it idly into the water, and we watched it negotiate its way, slithering round a rock till it joined the flow beyond. We enjoyed a few minutes of uncompetitive Pooh sticks as the late afternoon sun glinted off the little white peaks of the water, watching the bigger sticks make their way into the distance. There was no need to speak. When the sun dropped and it grew too cool to sit any longer, we made our way back through a landscape suddenly bleached of colour.

Joe turned to me. "Content?"

"With this silence? Mmm, yes," and we grinned at each other.

As we approached his house, Joe asked after Suzie, and I felt on safer ground. I told him about B&BQs and waxed lyrical about her success.

Joe smiled as he took off his boots. "I love your enthusiasm, Orbs. Aren't you jealous?"

I gawped at him. "Of her success? No, absolutely not. I love it."

"Of what, then?"

I fell silent. "I'd rather not talk about it." There was a limit to how much could be said.

My lack of response seemed to bring things to a halt. We said little as I gathered up my things. But before we left the cottage Joe stood still, as if he'd made up his mind.

"What is it, Orbs? What's bugging you? You might as well tell me what you've come all this way to say."

Oh God. What could I say? I hadn't thought it through, so what came tumbling out was a turbulent flood of confused thoughts and pent-up emotion. About the bank and how I hated it. About my love of fooling, and of Suze. About money, about secrets, about frustrated ambitions and about my feelings of unworthiness. When I finally came to a halt, I averted my head in embarrassment.

Joe's response was kind enough. He patted me on the back and wished me well, but he was my teacher, after all. In his usual forthright manner, he'd shone a light on the realities of my life, and I didn't like what I saw. I'd hoped that some time with Joe would cheer me up, that he might have some ideas of what I might do, but I left feeling low. I was miserable. I was living a dishonest life. I didn't tell the truth to others, and I didn't tell the truth to myself.

I stopped on the way back for a snifter. I felt I deserved a treat, and was defiant as I came into the flat. Suzie was lying on the settee, reading. She looked up and then down again at her book. She could always smell the booze. I felt unreasonably angry, and responded by taking a beer out of the fridge.

Chapter 7

"Morning all."

"Morning, Orbs."

I couldn't avoid it; it was time to go back to the bank. When I was there I fell into this formal stylised way of speech. We were probably all pretending but it seemed to be generally expected. My parents would have been sorely disappointed by my colleagues. Apart from the partners, Hooray Henrys they were not. Perfectly ordinary blokes from Essex, Kent, you name it, but not Oxbridge. The only public-school chaps I was still in touch with worked in prime brokerage – investing millions for the poor little rich boys who couldn't do it for themselves.

I didn't care what my colleagues thought of me, because they didn't know me. They probably resented me coming and going: a tosser foisted on them by the powers that be. Since I went to school with the son of one of the partners, that had a grain of truth, but in fact the only times I'd ascended to the dizzy heights of Ralph's thick pile office were on my appointment, and for my annual review. At opposite ends of the organisation, both geographically and organisationally, our paths rarely crossed. He never commented on our connection and I just kept my head down, did what I was told and raked in the dough at the end of the month.

For this was a work day, not a fool day but a stupid day, a pretend day. Fooling isn't pretending. Quite the opposite. It's being me. Being. With a space around me. Sometimes when I'm walking or cycling, I manage to take that space along with me but usually all that busyness, all that media stuff coming at me, floods the space. At the bank there's no space, just pointless busyness. I was tempted to bring in my Monopoly set next time I went, but I doubted they would get the point.

I got up quietly so as not to disturb Suzie. She'd been doing a gig the night before, and was late in. On my City days I had to be in at eight, so that was the middle of the night for her. I put on my one and only posh suit, bought for speech days at school and hanging loose on me now. I really needed to get a new one but that would be to confirm that I actually did this job and, besides, I couldn't afford it. I knew Suze would have bought it for me in a flash – had offered, in fact – but I was damned if I'd take her money for something so insignificant.

It did feel like the crack of dawn. Like most in the entertainment business, we're used to going to bed in the early hours and getting up late. Still, it didn't take me long to get there. It's only just over two miles, and with the new cycle superhighways a much easier ride, though not without its dangers, especially as you get near Bank. Car drivers can be such prats. There are slightly more interesting routes, but my priority, both in getting to work and coming home, is to get it over with as quickly as possible. Not my favourite kind of cycling.

I'm a pretty legal sort of cyclist. I don't ride on the pavement and, unless seriously frustrated, I don't jump the lights or go the wrong way down one-way streets. However, I can lose my rag. On one occasion, when I was nearly run down by a car cutting in front of me to turn left, I banged hard on the roof of his car. I then had to spend the next twenty minutes or so frantically zigzagging my way through some back streets to avoid his retaliation. But he could have killed me.

Not only did I have to pretend to be someone other than I am to work there, I'd had to make up a story of what I did the rest of the time. I had alighted on the idea of teaching. A maths teacher, that would do: worthy and badly paid. Another lie, another betrayal. For someone who sets such store by authenticity, I had developed a fine line in fabrication.

FREDDIE

Chapter 8

Voices have played too great a part in my life. My brother hears them. Has done since he was a kid, and he still lives at home. He talks to people in the street, which for such buttoned-up people as Mum and Dad is absolutely mortifying. I think they wonder what they've done to deserve it. No wonder they have needed to feed him pills to shut him up, damp him down. Freddie is the handsome one; he's always attracted the girls, until he goes weird, and even then, some cling on, positive that they can help.

"Where's Freddie?" was the recurrent refrain of my childhood. My parents have always been so anxious, always looking out for my big brother, who had a tendency to disappear. My big schizo brother. To be frank, they had every reason to be anxious. Although Freddie was never violent towards himself or others, sometimes it was clear that his voices were punishing, scornful, angry. I have a strong childhood memory of Freddie, aged about fifteen, clinging on to my father for dear life, a look of terror on his face. And my father helplessly patting him on the head. As the smaller child, it was hard not to be affected by his fear, but it was rare that I saw him like that. Mostly, he just sat around in a passive state, subdued (medicated, I now realise) or away (in hospital). Sometimes he talked to me in a way that was confusing, but I quickly learned to see the signs. My antennae were very acute, and I learned to steer clear. And my parents usually whisked him away without explanation, no doubt trying to protect me, but sometimes leaving behind them a bewildered little boy.

One way or another I just got the feeling that I didn't matter. Everyone was so caught up with the problem child that it was hard to be around, to feel my own presence, and I got out as soon as I could. He was the older one and I sometimes felt Mum and Dad had forgotten I'd arrived, and barely noticed when I left. It wasn't surprising that they didn't know what I was up to now.

And me? I coped. Did what was expected: posh school, posh job. Fortunately, they didn't expect me to go to uni; they cared more about my making a splash in the City. Just as well; though I have a facility for figures, I'm not the academic type. And they never knew I'd opted out. I suppose I could have shocked them into taking notice, but I couldn't be bothered with the fuss it would cause. Their ignorance suits me. They're happy with what they think I'm doing, and it means they leave me alone.

Although I couldn't wait to get out and certainly never regretted it, I did sometimes wonder how big brother Freddie was getting on. Perhaps now that everyone was at it on their phones, talking in the street was not such a big deal. And my parents were getting older. I tried not to think about that.

I knew that Suze was hurt that I hadn't introduced her to my family. I made it clear at the outset that we didn't get on, that I didn't see them, but I'm sure she still thought that I was somehow ashamed of her – she isn't from our class, after all. As if that mattered. I explained that I didn't want to share this precious part of my life with them, to sully it. I'm not sure she believed me, though it's the truth. As for Mum, when I had to phone on her birthday or whatever, she always asked and I always said, "No, no one special, Mum," and she always replied, "Time you settled down with a nice girl, Aubrey." Maybe she thought I was some sort of City lothario. As if.

So when Suzie picked up my phone the other day, she was as astonished as I was to hear who it was. "Hello? Who? Oh, *Freddie*, goodness, how nice." Freddie? What the heck? When had he ever rung me? "Yes, he's just coming out of the shower."

I wrapped myself in a towel and took the phone. "Hi Freddie. You okay? Good. In London? Well, er, yes, of course.

What a surprise. Come to supper." I hoped I hadn't sounded as grudging as I felt. As I put the phone down, Suzie looked at me with glowing eyes. She's a family girl at heart.

"You don't know how lucky you are," she would say. "If I had family here..."

But she didn't. Although we'd neither of us shared much about our families – neither happy, both painful – I did know that her mother had died when Suzie was ten, and that once she was through uni, her father had gone off to Australia with his second family. He'd been there for years, and didn't give a damn. I suppose I'm relatively lucky, but Suzie doesn't know the half of it. How my life would not be my own if my family were in it.

"How wonderful, Orbs. A chance to make up with your family." Turning to the ever-present creature on her left hand, "Isn't it, Bruce?"

"Hmm. Don't know about that."

"Oh, don't be such an old misery."

But for once Bruce and I were of one mind. "Mmm," I said, "Freddie's difficult, you know. Don't expect too much." In truth I was dreading his visit. Dreading the havoc my brother could cause in our blissful little nest. Why was he coming?

I explained to him how to get to our place. "It's pretty easy to find. Look for the dry cleaners. We're above that. Bell at the top of the stairs." It's not perfect, but we like the location – pretty good public transport and a few minutes' walk to everything we need. Great markets and there's even a good butcher (halal). I was brought up to be fussy about my meat. Suzie's vegetarian so we don't buy much. I just treat myself when she's away. We're renting, of course. There's no way we could get a mortgage with such an erratic lifestyle or for a flat above a shop. But as we've neither of us managed to accumulate much in the way of furniture it suits us, for now. It doesn't need much upkeep, and even if the landlord's pretty useless, at least if anything goes wrong it's his responsibility. It's just a one-bedder – well, officially two bedrooms, but one of them is only big enough for our junk. With such a small flat we have to keep it reasonably tidy, but I have to admit that comes more naturally to Suzie than to me. It's hard to find room for the clothes for our different lives; the fooling clothes and accessories live in the chest in our bedroom. I don't have that many for my other life – just a couple of suits and some shirts. Hard to be smart on a restricted budget.

Freddie was on time – he always is. I must say it was good to see him after, oh, I don't know how long. He looked good, maybe a little thicker round the waist, but his usual handsome self, and his eyes were bright. Those big appealing eyes that so often get him what he wants. Mine aren't anything special. A nice enough brown if you look hard enough, but too deep set. As usual, Freddie made me feel a scruff. It wasn't that he had smart clothes; he just wore them well.

As he entered the flat, he looked around him in wonder. I don't think he ever realised that people lived in places like this. Welcome to the real world, Bro. But then he recovered his manners.

"Hello, Orbs." It was good to hear his voice, his clear baritone voice, and I wondered if he still sang. We gave each other a well-bred brotherly half-hug and, in some embarrassment, clapped each other on the back.

He then held out his hand. "Hi, you must be Suzie. It's good to meet you. I'm Freddie. Though Gulliver's talking to me just now."

Suzie didn't blink but carried right on chatting to him while I got us all a drink.

"Are your parents well?"

"Yes, thank you, apart from Dad's hearing, which isn't very good."

Supper was an awkward affair – and, as it turned out, a rather gender-divided one. Freddie doesn't believe that green things are meant to be eaten, so there was a hefty chop on my and Freddie's plates, and for Suzie a delicate little platter of vegetables. Suzie did her best, but conversation was desultory, partly because I had no idea why Freddie had come, and was waiting to be told, but mainly because Freddie was transfixed by Bruce, who was back on Suzie's arm. The puppet's head was cocked, peering at my brother, who couldn't take his eyes off him.

At last he burst out, "Can you make him speak, Suzie? Would you show me?"

Suzie glanced at me. She knew I wouldn't like it, but I shrugged. I had no idea how Freddie would react. In for a penny. So, after the meal, she did.

I have to say that he was completely captivated. Whereas other men ogled Suzie, for Freddie the attraction was Bruce. He was mesmerised, and, glancing at Suzie to check her seeming lack of interest, and beguiled by the attention he was being paid, Freddie began to chat to the fox quite naturally, opening up in a way he rarely did with people. And, though I couldn't stand the way he talked to the puppet as if it was real, I had to admit that it seemed to make the evening go with a swing. As we drank our coffee and finished the wine, there was a real buzz of conversation. Though Suzie and I barely spoke, even between us there was communication. While Bruce and Freddie rabbitted away, Suzie's eyes sank ever deeper into mine. I don't know how she did it. It was completely bizarre, but even in this way it was good to have her attention. As she absent-mindedly stroked the nape of the puppet's sleek neck, it felt as if she were stroking me. It was extraordinarily erotic.

And, meanwhile, a surreal conversation continued in the background.

"Hello, Bruce, I'm Freddie."

"Hello, Freddie. Who are you?"

"Well, my full name is Frederick De'Ath Grimsby-Grenville."

"Quite a mouthful."

"Yes. That's why I'm Freddie. Who are you?"

"I'm just Bruce."

Pause.

"What do you do?"

"I speak, or rather Suzie speaks for me. I find it easier that way."

"Yes, I can see that. I have different voices too. They speak to me."

"What do they say?"

"Oh, I'm not allowed to tell you that."

I barely listened to what they were saying. I was too caught up in a pair of seductive hazel eyes.

But I was abruptly jerked into consciousness when Freddie turned to me and said, "Did I tell you, Orbs, that I've come off the pills?"

OMG. "What do Mum and Dad say?"

Freddie shook his copious locks. "Oh, they don't like it. They've never understood. But I feel so much better." It was true, he did look well, not so puffy, colour in his cheeks. "I heard about a café for people who hear voices."

"A cafe?" The mind boggled.

"And I plucked up my courage and went. Honestly, Orbs, it was great. I've never met a whole group of people who understand, people like me. So I'm going to the local network. Some of them are really laid back about their voices. They say they don't have psycho problems, don't get labelled. They hear voices and it's cool. So I'm fine with it too now. I feel much more myself." Mum and Dad must be shitting themselves – they always said it was only the pills that enabled them to cope.

Freddie turned back to Bruce. "I must say, it's good to have someone to talk to. Mum and Dad don't like me mentioning the voices. And other people won't listen at all. They think I'm mad."

"You don't seem mad to me." Despite his rasping voice I'd never heard Bruce sound so friendly. What was he up to? Maybe

Freddie's almost innocent responses had got under his guard. "Thanks. I'm getting better. This chap at the Maudsley seems to understand, so it's worth the trek up to London. The only voices I have now are Mavis and Gulliver and I'm cool with them. They usually keep quiet unless I'm really stressed. I understand so much more about why I have them. I take their advice but they don't mess my mind anymore. They're friends. I couldn't imagine my life without them."

All this was very interesting, no doubt, but I couldn't wait for my brother to leave. The moment the door shut behind him, I turned to find Suzie laying Bruce down on the sideboard. No interfering bedtime ritual, no lullaby, just love and lust then and there on the carpet. Stupendous!

We saw more of Freddie after that. Extending an invitation to him was like a code: an invitation for ourselves to the rampant sex that we knew would follow. So weird, when I look back on it, but it seemed to work for all of us. I sometimes felt that we were using my brother, but we had regained our passion for each other and Freddie, poor chap, had gained a new friend.

Our parents were apparently pleased at their sons' rapprochement. I don't know what Freddie told them – he's never been able to keep anything to himself – but I had to find a way to keep them from descending on us. At all costs. I fantasised about endowing Suzie with some terrible deformity that would make my hypersensitive mother quail. "Oh, Aubrey," she would say, "I'm not sure I could cope with that. My nerves, you know." I did know. They had been my childhood companions. And as for Bruce – God knows what they thought. "A fox?" – another of his delusions, presumably. But Freddie had begun to paint again, and was earning a bob or two as a jobbing gardener. There were signs of progress.

When my mother rang on Bank Holiday Monday, the conversation took a predictable turn. "Frederick tells us that you've found yourself a lovely girl at last. I'm so glad, darling."

"Suzie, yes, Mother. Sorry, I should have mentioned it, but the fact is that Suzie is terribly shy and really doesn't like meeting people."

"It's funny, Frederick didn't mention that."

"Oh, you know what Freddie's like."

"Yes." And she sighed. There was a wealth of sadness in that "yes", and for a moment I felt bad.

There was actually a glimmer of truth in what I had told her. Suzie isn't shy – of course not, how could she be in that profession? – but she is quite reserved about her private life (thank God). To her agent's dismay she avoids interviews when she can. "They always want to psychoanalyse me. 'So, tell me, Belinda, do you find that Bruce channels your negative feelings?' 'Does Bruce express parts of you that you can't otherwise express?'" Indeed, Suzie's agent is employed as much to keep the media off her back as to get publicity. To strip any coverage of any muck-raking potential; to keep it innocuous without appearing as if there's something to hide. Not an easy task.

But Mother was still talking.

"Frederick tells me that the flat you're living in is really small. Above a shop, he said, can that be right? Surely it's time you found somewhere more befitting your status."

Whatever that is. Not what she imagines, that's for sure. In fact, we were thinking of moving, but that was because of Suzie's success, not mine. I really needed to put more effort into getting some gigs. The problem was that the more time I spent at the bank, making enough money to live on, the less time I had to find money-making work that I really wanted to do. Vicious circle.

But I didn't spend much time agonising about that. I was too caught up in the flowering of my relationship with Suzie. I hadn't realised how dull, how unstimulating, our lives had become, until this injection of excitement. We really had been on the brink. It was more than rediscovery: sex was better than it had ever been. It was as if our creative energies had come together and were being channelled into something very new and very special. Sometimes Suzie had to call a halt. She had a show to prepare for, after all, and needed to get some sleep.

But we were energised and, even with all Suzie's preparations, we found time to enjoy the long summer days. I suggested an outing.

"Shall we go to the park? Have a picnic? Have we got anything in?"

So we raided the fridge and threw into a knapsack some cheese, a packet of ham that was only just past its sell-by date, a couple of apples, muesli bars, some bottles of water (and one of beer), and decided to buy some rolls on the way. Suzie sat back down at the table to finish her coffee.

I tweaked her ear. "Come on, lazy bones. It's a lovely day."

Suzie shook me off. "You're a fine one to talk. You're still in your pyjamas."

"I bet I'm ready first!" Suzie sprang to her feet and we both scrambled to find some clothes, colliding in the doorway and mock-fighting to get into the bathroom, squeezing sexily against each other and splashing each other with water. I'm not sure how much washing went on, and we nearly didn't make it past the bedroom but, eventually, breathless and laughing, we found ourselves running down the street to Mile End Park.

* * *

The next time Freddie came, I arrived home later than I'd expected, and my brother was ensconced on the settee, talking to Suzie and Bruce. I'd forgotten it was Freddie's London day.

I took off my coat and threw it on a chair.

"Hi folks. Sorry I'm late."

"Where have you been?"

"Oh, just for a walk and I lost sense of time."

"What he means," said Bruce, "is that he's been walking the labyrinth." I gave Suzie a quick look of annoyance but she was seemingly oblivious.

Freddie turned to me with excitement, "A labyrinth?"

"Yes, do you know what they are? They..."

"Oh, I know what a labyrinth is. We had one at the hospital."

"Really? In the garden?"

"No, they brought it into the meeting room."

I was puzzled, then realised he meant a cloth one. I'd never seen one, though I knew they existed.

"Yes, Miriam came with me."

"Miriam?"

"Yes, one of my voices. She's left me now." He looked a little doleful, then perked up at the memory. "I loved it. A whole bunch of us walked it."

"Together?"

"Yes, we followed each other round and met each other on the way."

Sounded like my idea of hell.

"So," said Freddie with excitement, "there's one near here?"

"Yes, on the earth and in the grass."

"Wicked! Can we go and do it?"

"Maybe next time, Freddie. Supper's ready and I'm bushed."

Why did Suzie have to go and mention it? Maybe it's selfish, but I don't, I absolutely don't, want to share my precious place with my brother.

Chapter 9

Meanwhile, preparations for the big day rumbled on, with Suzie scurrying hither and thither and keeping erratic hours. I kept my head down, trundling off to the bank from time to time, and occasionally chatting to my fellow fools to keep myself sane.

In any case, it was time I got back into my own real work. Hoping to absent myself both from the hassle at home but mostly from the nonsensical job at the bank, I took the opportunity to get back on the festival circuit. I couldn't wait to see my mates. Now that most of my work is on my own, I must say I miss the others. There's nothing better than feeling you're all part of a bigger whole, sometimes staying in the same digs, having a laugh and a common moan. And after the show relaxing in the pub.

Festivals are a doddle. Everyone there is determined to enjoy themselves and, in that atmosphere, everyone lets their hair down. Anything goes. July is a high point of the festival year, with a lot of players flexing their muscles before Edinburgh. I had booked myself in towards the end of the Guildford Fringe – unpaid, but near enough to London to make it workable, and good to get the juices working again. I'd agreed to do the Green Man, something I'm comfortable and familiar with, which brings its own challenge of keeping it fresh and spontaneous – as usual, there's no planning allowed. But it means I don't have to fuss about a new costume or anything. This one – "the Morris dancer without bells" outfit, as Suzie rudely calls it – entails yards of green plastic leaves wound round my body, which I got from a local pound shop, and some murky-looking camouflage trousers and top from Camden Lock. There's plenty of cheap stuff around, if you look for it. I took it carefully out of the chest, and wrapped it in cloth before putting it in my rucksack. Costumes and red noses are precious. As usual I travelled by train, with my tent on my back. With no car, I have to manage without a set and the bare minimum of props.

The set for this act is the natural world (no venue cost!), and in the Castle Grounds there was a perfect flat clearing between the trees with room for seating at one end. The public could come and go, so I wasn't allowed to make an official charge, but I hoped that my battered old hat strategically placed at the entrance might encourage donations. Sadly, my show didn't attract many people. Because the booking had been last minute, the act hadn't appeared on the festival programme, so I had been reduced to scrabbling around to get some flyers printed and handing them out during the day. And, for late July, the weather was foul: rainy, muddy, boggy. Even with a couple of benches at the far end, there weren't too many people who wanted to huddle up in their coats to watch a strange figure prancing about in the woods.

I had hoped for shadows and the dappled sunlight of a summer evening, but even on an overcast day I was able to make the most of the weather. The dim light meant that my appearance from behind an oak was a gradual one, as my leafy shape slowly separated itself from the outline of the tree. Communicating with the audience is everything, and in a silent practice such as ours, the connection is often a subtle one.

I stepped slowly and deliberately into a patch of soft mud, noticing and enjoying the disgusting delicious sucking sound as the mud sought to retain my foot, and then released it suddenly with a plop. I looked at the audience to check that they were enjoying it. They were, so I did it again. And again. Glug plop, glug plop. They laughed. I looked at my foot, and then at the audience. Up down, up down. If it works, milk it. Less is more.

I was pleased with how my show went and it was good to get back into the harness, but for once I didn't really enjoy the festival as a whole. Some of the friends I'd been hoping to see were away, at bigger festivals or on gigs here and there. All doing more than me. Those who were there asked, of course, after Suzie, and I had to give her excuses, without explaining why she wasn't there.

It was so frustrating that even in the one place where I can usually relax, in the one world where Suzie's alter ego is no secret, I wasn't allowed to let on. It's only when we are with our own crowd that we can be open about who we really are. Suzie too has appearances to keep up when she goes into the office, but at least it's real work that she believes in and, as she's freelance, they just assume that she's just working from home or elsewhere. I can't help feeling that our secrecy might protect our privacy, but it cuts us off from our friends.

Though I often like being on my own, this time it wasn't the same without Suze. Even when we're doing different things during the day, we're used to getting together at night. The tent is a lonely place without her. It's a squash for two, but miserably large for just one. As a rule, when we're apart, we try to speak every evening, but on the first two nights all I got was Suzie's voicemail – that crisp business-like tone: "Hello, this is Suzie Tavener. Sorry I can't take your call" – so that by the time I got through I was pretty disgruntled. But when I finally got through and heard the pleasure in her voice, any irritation dissolved.

"Oh, Orbs, how nice. How are you?"

"Fine. Tiny house, but a good one." I shared news of some of our mutual friends. "Naturally they're all asking after you, but I can't say much, can I? How's it going?"

And, of course, that's what she really wanted to talk about. Even my cool Suzie found it hard to contain her excitement.

"You'll never guess who they've got for the first show."

"No, who?"

"Only David Cameron."

"Bloody hell. A bit out of it, isn't he?"

"But he's got a lot to answer for. A lot of people are very angry with him. Clearing off like that."

"I'm amazed he agreed."

"Wants to 'set the record straight', I guess. He's been out of the spotlight for quite a while. Maybe he sees an opportunity to engage with a new generation of voters."

"Well, I can't wait to see you make mincemeat of him."

She laughed. "In the nicest possible way."

I must say, she is very even-handed. I don't know how she manages to suppress her own political views.

"Oh, darling Suze, I do miss you."

"Me too. When are you coming home?"

"Oh, not sure. You know how it is. Things crop up." Feeling I had to make a stand for my independence somehow, I was deliberately vague.

I hung up, feeling lonelier than ever. Talk about cutting off my nose. Of course I'd rather be at home.

Chapter 10

But when I did get back I found that nothing had changed. Suzie was busier than ever, and out most of the time. But even if the festival had been a bit of a letdown, I felt nourished by spending some time with others of like mind. Sometimes it's a pain being on my best behaviour.

Although Suzie is a social animal, it's always on her own terms. She's never hung out with the late-night drinkers – I suppose she's seen enough of the boozing culture among journalists. The fact that she's not one of the crowd doesn't seem to bother her. She and Bruce, performance, her place on the stage – those are enough for her. She's not keen on social media either. Jessie has made her go on Twitter, but it's all a bit half-hearted. Though she has thousands of followers, she rarely tweets herself. Jessie has set up a Facebook page for B&BQs, but it's she that keeps it updated, not Suzie.

Come to think of it, chatty and friendly though she is, in the work arena Suzie's a loner. Some vents work with others, even manipulating the same puppet with someone else – one taking the legs, another the beak or mouth. Suzie could never see the point. I guess she likes doing her own thing, being in control. Despite her charm and popularity, she doesn't rely on them. Her air of self-containment is real: she doesn't seem to need other people. She doesn't even go to vent festivals. At the beginning, eager to learn, she did. But now she just sees her show as a form of self-expression. She finds it liberating to use another voice. But it's as well as, not instead of, her own.

But sometimes she lets go and allows her social self to blossom. With her friends, even for work when she has to, she can charm the birds from the trees.

"Oh, Orbs," she called, as I came in from work and parked my bike in the hall, "are you free on the twentieth?"

I took off my helmet. "I think so. Nothing I can think of. I should be around. Why?"

"They're throwing a launch party."

"Oh, no."

"Come on, Orbs, I know it's not your idea of fun, and I don't usually ask, but this is important. It's a big thing for me. If you're never around, people won't believe I've got a partner."

So I could hardly refuse.

"And, besides," said Suzie coyly, picking an invisible thread from the sleeve of my jacket, "there may be useful people there."

"*Useful?*"

"Oh, come on, you know what I mean. People who might have a gig for you, or something."

Maybe that's why I'm not doing well. I'm just no good at this sort of thing.

I arrived late at the club, because, as Suzie's – Belinda's – partner, I knew I wouldn't be able to leave early. The noise hit me as soon as I opened the door of the club, and increased as I walked across to the cellar entrance. I stood at the top of the stairs, took a deep breath, and plunged in. The room was packed full of animated figures, glass of red or white in hand, penguin waiters squeezing through to offer trays of delicate little mouthfuls of this and that. People shouting to make themselves heard and the four-piece jazz band in the corner. The lights were dim, but at least there was no haze of smoke any more.

Some women had obviously come straight from work and some had dressed for the occasion, looking as if they had never worked in their lives. The men, well, as usual their garb was pretty unremarkable: suits, sweaters, the occasional tie. Dressed up, dressed down. I had toyed with the idea of coming in costume, but then I would have had to behave accordingly, and that wouldn't have gone down well. BBC people, some show biz friends. Not a fool in sight. But I wore odd socks, just to keep my end up.

Wishing I were taller, I looked around for Suzie. She managed to spot me, and waved enthusiastically. She was wearing a little (and I do mean little) number in red and black. Her cheeks were pink, and she was celebrating in style. The start of the series, and, we all assumed, the first of many. Suzie gave me a hug, and gestured to a podgy middle-aged man standing next to her. "Geoff, have you met my partner, Orbs?" and, then, quietly, behind her hand, "Don't forget, you two, that here I'm Belinda. Orbs, all this is thanks to Geoff. He's the one who thought up the idea." She flashed us a smile and moved on.

Oh, yes, the political editor. We shook hands. "Good to meet you," he said in sonorous tones. You could tell he was used to addressing the nation.

"You must be very pleased," I murmured.

He was enjoying the view of Suzie's back as she wove her way through the room. "Sorry?"

"YOU MUST BE VERY PLEASED." It didn't improve with repetition.

"Ah, yes. I'm delighted. I always knew it would work. She's such a talented young woman."

We were interrupted by the speeches, given by the producer, Emily, and Jessie, with suitably professional superlatives. And then "Belinda" took the mic, and everyone cheered. I basked in reflected glory (and wished, not for the first time, that I had some glory of my own). Suzie was completely irresistible, as always. And I get to take her home.

But not yet. If I have to be at a party at all, I prefer to make an impression, and then leave while it is still in full swing. "Always leave them wanting more." But tonight Belinda would have to stay until the last drink-sodden guest petered out, and that meant that I couldn't leave either.

I watched Suzie as she worked the room. She was sparkling and chatty, and happy to share herself with friends, the eager press, everyone in the room. She was in her element, and it was clear to me that I was not.

As befits a celebrity, we took a cab home, and I had to stop myself looking to see if we were being followed. Do the press have any way of finding out where Belinda lives?

Chapter 11

There was barely time to breathe before the first night was upon us. For months it had seemed as if it would never come, and then, suddenly, straight after the bank holiday, it was there. So far we hadn't been assailed by the media. We'd been right in thinking that the *Strictly* announcements would preoccupy the papers and the public. But once the series took off, the spotlight would be on it. The Beeb's publicists would make sure of that.

Suzie didn't sleep much the night before but, bright as a button, with Bruce and her props in her bag, she was up and ready for the car that would take her to the studio for 8:00 a.m.

"*8:00 a.m.?* You've got to be joking. Why on earth do they need you at such an ungodly hour?"

"They did last time. Don't you remember? But it's not for me. It's for the director, the floor manager, camera people and everyone else. Lighting have to be in there even earlier. You've no idea what goes into a show – even a simple one like this."

"Sounds like lunacy to me. I bet Cameron won't be there at 8:00 a.m."

"Oh no, of course not. They'll use someone else all day to sit in for him. Then he'll swan in this evening. Anyway," she gave me a peck on the cheek, "must go."

I hugged her ferociously. "Good luck, darling. Break a leg, or whatever."

It was a strange day. I had no idea what to do. Trying to make the most of the sunshine, I went for a brief cycle ride along the canal, but didn't want to stay out in case – in case what? Just felt I needed to be in the flat, so I got out a boxed set of *The Wire* and sat in front of it, again.

Suzie rang me at lunchtime.

"Hi Suze, all okay?"

"Yes, fine. It's all a bit tedious, really. Doing stuff over and over again to get the lighting, the camera angles right. We've spent so much time on the timing. You remember last time it was a bit of an issue. That's the thing about live TV, you have to get it right."

"I can imagine."

"But everyone's been great. Everyone's on it, completely focussed, all the time. Amazing."

I couldn't settle to anything, endlessly checking my emails, picking up a book and putting it down, counting the hours until the show came on. Suzie hadn't sounded too nervous. It must help that she's done it before, even if it was months ago.

The programme was a triumph. Cameron was held to task about Brexit, with Bruce jeering, "You really landed Theresa in it, didn't you? Running away like that." Cameron was, of course, used to the barracking of PMQs but nothing had prepared him for this, and when he turned on his attacker, the audience laughed. Attacking a fox, a puppet! How ridiculous. Who else could have made him such a laughingstock? None of the clever parliamentarians, not even a Paxman or a Humphries, could make such a mockery of a former prime minister. Cameron could hardly attack Belinda, sweetly smiling Belinda, from under her blond curls. The overall impression was of acute frustration and, yes, powerlessness. It made you wonder why these people put themselves through it. Like Farage or the Hamiltons on *Have I Got News for You?* Did they imagine they were immune? Or that any publicity was worth it? Goodness knows what B&B might make of Tony Blair.

Suzie came in in the early hours, flushed with success, trying not to wake me. As she entered the bedroom, even through barely open eyes, I took in her radiant loveliness. A dream-like apparition. "Wonderful, darling," I slurred. "Well done. Sorry, sleepy. Talk in the morning? Come to bed. You must be shattered."

I was asleep again before she joined me. She was usually high after her performances, and took a while to come down, often sitting with a coffee, chatting to Bruce, settling him and herself before succumbing to sleep.

The following week I was visiting an out-of-town client so, knowing I wouldn't make it back in time for the show, I made a point of stopping off at a Stratford pub. I ordered a pint and chicken in the basket and joined a sizeable group in the lounge, many leaning back against the bar to watch. B&B's guest this time was the young SNP MP who caused a by-election sensation when she overturned the huge majority of a Tory predator. Bruce kept up his scandalising reputation, rasping out: "How is it being a young woman in the Commons now, Ellie? Any trouble with the dirty old men?"

Belinda's shocked "*Bruce!*" was almost drowned out by the delighted roar from the young studio audience and from the pub. As the fox stared out into the room with an air of nonchalant innocence, Ellie held her composure.

"A good question. It's not easy being in such a male environment, but now that it's all more in the open and there are new channels for complaint, I think there's less of it about."

It was good to be with others. I felt such a sense of pride, watching Suzie, and watching her audience. I hugged my connection to myself. If only they knew!

This second show made even more of a splash than the first. Suzie was sailing pretty close to the wind and you could see why they'd given the show a later-night slot. Of course, it was nothing compared with what's regularly aired in working men's clubs, but then audiences there aren't counted in millions, including the country's movers and shakers. It was fortunate that public attention was caught by the revelations rather than those who had triggered them. Keeping herself out of the picture is part of Suzie's skill.

But I felt that it was only a matter of time before the secrecy bubble burst. Already Belinda's name was being bandied about, even by the more serious papers. Even the *Guardian* magazine was asking: "Is ventriloquism making a comeback?"

The morning after the second show, after very little sleep, Suzie was woken by the phone. It was a long call. I was having breakfast and didn't hear what was said, but it sounded acrimonious.

A somewhat grumpy Suzie emerged from the bedroom.

"What was that about?"

"That was Emily. There have been some complaints about last night. She asked me – no, told me – to keep a lid on it. BBC standards, blah, blah."

I knew better than to say anything.

"I know Bruce is outrageous, but there's nothing I can do about it. They don't seem to understand that I have no control over what comes out of his mouth. If they want B&B, that's what they'll get. And, given the ratings, they should be grateful. And could phone at a less unearthly hour." She stomped back to bed. It took quite a lot to make Suzie cross. She usually left it to Bruce.

As usual after a show, we tried to have a quiet day, but it was filled up with mostly congratulatory messages, not least from Jessie, who was over the moon. "That was terrific, darling, even better than last time. You should see the Twitter feed. It's beyond viral."

Chapter 12

Thursday morning. Suzie had gone off for lunch to debrief with Emily, and I was in my dressing gown, standing mindlessly in front of an open fridge. When the phone rang, I had to fumble under all the papers on the kitchen table to find it.

"Hello?"

"Mr Grenville?"

"Yes?"

"Hello. I'm ringing from St Thomas's hospital."

"What?"

"It's Ms Tavener."

"Suzie?"

"Don't worry, sir, she's not seriously hurt, but she's had a fall and we're just taking a look. We thought you'd like to know."

"What happened? How bad is she?"

"She tripped over a paving stone. She's hurt her wrist, so we're doing some X-rays and so on. And she banged her head. She seems fine in herself but we need to keep an eye on her. The thing is, sir," she paused, "she seems unable to speak. Is that usual?"

"Not speaking? Er, no, not at all usual. Can I see her?"

"Yes, of course."

Unable to speak? Must be the shock. Later, I wondered how they'd known to contact me, but it turned out they'd asked for her next of kin and she'd written my name. *Written* it! They'd decided to keep her in overnight, just to keep an eye on her and make sure she wasn't concussed.

I hardly knew how I got there, but when I arrived, Suzie was in bed in a ward, lying on her side, facing away from the door and curled up in the foetal position. She didn't stir when I came in. She didn't speak.

"Hi Suze, it's me."

I sat on the bed (forbidden), and put the box of chocs down beside her.

She showed no sign of recognition. I longed to take her in my arms, but the remote quality of her stillness stopped me.

I went to the nurses' station just outside the ward. "I wonder whether you can help me. My name's Aubrey Grenville. I'm Suzie Tavener's partner. Could you tell me what happened?"

The young woman looked up from her computer and smiled. "Hello. Well, I was actually here when she was brought in. The paramedics said that she tripped on a kerbstone. Such bad luck. She fell awkwardly on to her outstretched hand, and hit her head." The nurse looked a little awkward, and said, "Of course, she hasn't been able to tell us anything directly." No.

"Will she be all right?"

"Oh, I'm sure she will. She might even be able to go home tomorrow. We're doing some X-rays and tests and just waiting for the doctor to see her in the morning. If you come back then, he'll be able to tell you more."

I went back into the ward and just sat on the bed, burbling about this and that for half an hour, then kissed her and left her to rest. I went home to an empty flat, and wept.

In the morning I went in first thing and hung around the ward until the doctor was free. She told me that because Suzie had hit her head, they'd done a CT scan but there was no sign of any damage. They'd thought that an operation on her wrist might be needed, but X-rays showed that there were no complications. Yes, she'd broken a couple of little bones in her wrist, but the bones had not been displaced, and a cast would do the trick. Once she'd been bound up, Suzie could go home.

"What about her not speaking?"

The doctor was reassuring. "I expect it's the shock. It should pass soon. If not, do ask your GP about it."

I went with Suze to the fracture clinic, sat with her as they plastered up her arm, the nurse prattling kindly to us both as she did so, then I collected her medicines from the pharmacy and bought us both some sandwiches from the cafe. It all took hours. I was completely at a loss.

Suzie's silence seemed to be that of someone not physically unable to speak but unwilling to engage. I called a taxi, waited for another half hour or so and finally took her home. In the taxi, Suzie sat with her left elbow on her knee, holding her immobilised wrist upright, as she'd been told. I held her other hand the whole way, and found myself talking to her as if to a child or demented old person. But she barely looked at me. And she didn't speak. I cooked us some supper, which she left untouched, helped her undress and get into bed, then sat in the sitting room with my head in my hands.

Only then did the question arise: where was Bruce?

I leapt from my chair and rifled through the grey plastic sack that we'd brought back from the hospital. There, at the bottom, was the limp little fox. Never had I been so pleased to see him. It was extraordinary that Suzie hadn't sought him out. I took him into the bedroom, and gently laid him on the pillow beside her. Maybe, when she woke, that would make all the difference.

But it didn't. Suzie showed no sign of even noticing him. Nothing could have told me more clearly how bad things were. After three days of continuing silence I took her to our GP. He examined her but could find nothing physically wrong. He gave her some anti-depressants (which I'm sure she didn't take) and advised her to rest. I took time off work and tried to look after her, but she refused to be babied. Whenever I tried to insist on anything she just turned on me with those newly fierce eyes. And said nothing.

I rang Freddie to let him know about her accident.

His first question was, "Which hand?"

"Left, not her dominant, fortunately. They say it might take months."

"But that means...How terrible."

Bruce. Of course. It hadn't occurred to me. As for many puppeteers, Suzie's puppet arm was not her dominant one.

And then all my anxiety and confusion burst out of me. "Bloody Bruce. Is that all you think about? Suze's been in an awful accident. She's in terrible pain, and all you can think of is that bloody, godforsaken, damned puppet."

There was a silence at the end of the line, then a little wavering voice. "Don't. Don't talk like that. Just don't," and the line went dead.

Oh God. Now I had to feel bad about Freddie too. I began to ring his number, then stopped. Better let him get over the shock. And anyway, I was still pretty angry. That wretched puppet was still in the way, always centre stage, even now.

Obviously the series was finished. Even if Suzie were miraculously to recover her powers of speech, with the state of her arm there was no way she could handle Bruce.

Chapter 13

In the morning, the doorbell rang. I wasn't dressed for visitors, nor was I in any state to receive them. As I opened the door, I pulled my tatty dressing gown about my nakedness and tried to look at ease.

Jessie swept in without a greeting, in one of her hallmark long full-skirted dresses, her white shoulder-length frizz streaked with purple. You did not mess with Jessie. She made the flat look small.

I plumped up the cushions in a nervous attempt to improve the look of the place.

"So, where is she?"

I motioned towards the bedroom. Jessie took one look inside, then came back out and sat down. "So, what's the story?"

"What story?"

"What are we going to say?"

"Well," I said weakly, "that she's had an accident and she's sick."

Jessie shook her head. "That won't do."

"They'll understand. If she's damaged her arm, she obviously can't go on."

"But if they can't speak to her, they'll cook up all sorts of stories about mental health, drugs, you name it. We can't have that. Emily is already having kittens because she can't get hold of her. If they've got to cancel, they'll have to find something else fast."

"Yes. Oh, I don't know, Jessie. I'm too worried about Suzie to give a toss about the rest. Isn't that your job?"

"Thank you for reminding me. But we have to make sure our stories tally, because they're bound to get on to you, if they haven't already?"

I shook my head. "All I would say if they rang is that she's too ill to talk to anyone. Which is the truth." And I'd had enough of lies.

Jessie stood up. "Well, we'll have to see what can be done. But for God's sake keep your mouth shut." And, with hair and dress streaming behind her, she left. I sat down again, feeling rather weak. Jessie was at the sharp end, of course, and probably right, but just now Suzie's career was the least of my concerns.

Even so, that afternoon I dug out Suzie's diary. I felt a heel, but we had to know if there were any appointments to deal with. And then I had to root about to find a number for George to ask about Vox Pop. He didn't know me from Adam, but he couldn't have been nicer, sending his best wishes to Suzie and wishing her a speedy recovery. It was good to hear that there were several columns in the bag, so there was no worry in the short term. If there was a long term, we'd have to deal with it then. Day by day.

The press was, of course, full of random theories about the reasons for the cancellation of the series and the circumstances of Belinda's disappearance. But with Jessie and the Beeb keeping to their promised silence about Belinda's whereabouts, we were mercifully left alone. Amid speculation, as Jessie had feared, about Belinda's mental health, even death, there was one version that swept away the rest. I don't know how the story started, but I first saw it in the *Mirror*:

BBC axes B&BQs: Vent Queen too hot to handle

Then a typical swipe in the *Standard*:

No 10 denies muzzling B&BQs

Poor old BBC. But I couldn't be sorry the pundits had got the wrong end of the stick. It took the pressure off us. I did wonder about Jessie's complicity. There wasn't much she wouldn't do to protect her clients' interests.

THE SILENCE DIARIES

I'm in shock too. No one seems to realise that. In desperation, and because there's no one I can share it with, I've begun to keep this little diary. It's just a way of jotting things down at the end of the day. Or the middle of the night.

Monday
How empty the flat seems, without Suzie's bright and cheerful chatter. I didn't realise how much it's filled my life. Nothing seems the same.

Tuesday
This is a house of mourning. A pall of silence has descended on the flat. I can't tell you what it's like, living with that – seemingly accusing – silence. It's as if someone's died. I tiptoe around, and when people ring my mobile or, desperate to get hold of Suzie, the almost disused landline, I find myself whispering, and self-conscious about any noise I make: the clatter of dishes as I put them away, or the flushing of the lavatory. As if I'm interrupting something. I'm suddenly aware of the small noises from outside – the sirens, muffled bumps from the flat next door, the murmur of voices from the dry cleaners below, sometimes the birds in the trees. And inside, the hum of the fridge, the ticking of the kitchen clock, and even the sound of my breathing. I'm more aware of tunes replaying themselves in my head, sometimes humming them under my breath, but scared of being overheard.

When I leave the house for a few minutes, everything outside is so loud. I can now understand why people might want to wear headphones, but of course they aren't using them to block out the noise, but to add to it.

Friday
I should be grateful for the peace and quiet – God knows I've yearned for it. But actually I hate being at home. I don't know what to do with

myself. I'm not used to sitting round the flat all the time, and can't summon up the energy to catch up with all the boring stuff I know needs doing. I'm drinking more than's good for me, but what else is there to do? My mind won't stop, so blotting it out is at least one alternative. Yes, I know there are better ones, but I'm not up to making the effort. I took Suzie to the GP last week – "nothing physically wrong" – and today to the psychiatrist. He's a nice enough man, with a pleasantly avuncular manner. He greeted us both, then asked Suzie if she would be able to write down her responses. She nodded.

When he asked, "Would you like your partner to come in with you?" she shook her head vigorously. I was devastated. I sat in the waiting room, vacantly leafing through magazines. I wanted to know what Suzie was writing, wanted to know what it was all about, above all why she was shutting me out. What had I done wrong? Eventually she came out and I took her home. There was nothing to be said.

It's known as selective mutism. I looked it up. It's a recognised condition, often post-traumatic. The loss of her connection with Bruce would certainly be classed as trauma: it's like uprooting a part of her body. The doctor reassured me that all the routine investigations are normal, and since Suzie can communicate by writing and follow commands given to her, he's pretty clear that there's no physiological damage. He obviously can't understand why such a minor injury should cause such a reaction. I know only too well, but there's no way I'm going to enlighten him. It's for Suzie to do that, and I can hardly imagine that she will.

He was kind, obviously understood that I was under some strain, and patted me on the back. "I'm sure it'll pass, Mr Grenville. We will just have to be patient."

Well, the diagnosis is reassuring, I suppose, but it doesn't help us cope with our day-to-day lives. The cards and flowers flood in and, as I take Suzie here and there to her various appointments, she's at the same time obstinately passive and shockingly biddable. This isn't the Suzie I know.

Sunday
*This morning, in an attempt to distract Suzie, and to make life seem
more normal, I put the radio on, and last night tried TV with* News
at Ten, *but it was no good: the sound of voices thundering through the
silence felt like a desecration. When I sit in the sitting room, it's not
like being alone, because there's a brooding presence in the next room.
I'm constantly on the alert: I feel all the time that something's about
to happen. At night I lie awake with Suzie motionless in the bed beside
me. She seems to sleep a good deal of the time, or at least pretend to.
She certainly doesn't want to be touched.*

Monday
*Last night, in desperation, I took some bedding into the sitting room,
and lay down on the settee. I have to get some sleep. I wasn't worried
about disturbing Suzie – nothing seems to do that. It's me that is
disturbed by the presence in my bed of a being so loved and familiar,
physically present, but absent in every other way. I am tantalised by
the sight and smell of her. It's hard to keep my hands to myself.*

*I woke early with the sun streaming in through the windows, and
for a moment I wondered where I was. I'm used to waking up in new
places, but it takes a little time to adjust. If I'm going to continue to
sleep in here, I'll have to put something up to cover the windows. We
don't have any spare curtains, but the magician's cloak will do. Dark
and capacious, and with who knows what mysterious powers. God
knows we could do with them. I went into the bedroom and drew back
the curtains to let in the day. Hoping the sight of sunlight would work
its magic. But Suzie didn't stir.*

*I keep talking to her – it sounds vacuous and I feel very silly but
I hope my chat will keep something alive both in her and between us.*

Wednesday 24th September
*I've started to put the date on these entries to help me get a grip.
Normally, I'm all too glad to forget about time, but in this featureless
swamp, knowing the date at least stops me feeling I've lost it altogether.*

It's now almost two weeks since the accident. I've left Suzie for an hour or so now and then but she does seem a bit better, so today I went to work. I worried, of course I did, but the GP assures me that, apart from her wrist, there's nothing physically wrong. It's just her lassitude, her speechlessness – and those are still completely unexplained. Leaving breakfast on a tray and some sort of lunch on a plate in the fridge, I put on my suit and my helmet and carried my bike down the stairs. With Suzie unable to work, someone has to pay the bills. That meant I had to crawl to the bosses at the bank and ask for more work. They were unexpectedly delighted. I couldn't confess to needing the money, so yet again had to fabricate a story. I no longer know who I am.

On my way in from work, I bumped into Palash, locking up his car.

We smiled at each other.

"Hi, Palash. Okay?"

"Yes, fine, thanks. You?"

He could see the answer in my face. "What's up?"

"Oh, it's Suzie, she's having a bad time. Hurt her wrist, and it's really got her down not being able to do things. It doesn't help that I need to work more at the moment."

"Oh, you should have said. I'll tell Hannah."

"Don't worry. We'll be fine." But I knew that his dear wife, five foot nothing and bustling with kindness, would be bringing round some of her delicious food. I didn't protest too much. Suzie could do with a treat (and so could I).

Friday 26th

I'm beyond worrying about what Hannah and Palash might think. I'm just relieved to know that they're on the case. I've been spending quite a lot of my evenings and days off organising a rota of friends to drop in, make sure Suzie eats, and encourage her to get up and dress. And talk to her. That's important. Her best mate, Rosemary, comes round every few days, bless her, and keeps me updated. As a friend from uni, she's known Suze a lot longer than me, and perhaps understands better what's going on, though there's nothing much to say about someone who won't speak. And who has switched off her phone. Her agent is beside herself. "What is the matter with her, Orbs? She just won't pick up. At this rate she'll kill off any chance of ever getting another booking."

"She's depressed, Jessie. She won't talk to me either."

"I despair." I could visualise her throwing up her hands at the other end of the phone. "There's only so much damage limitation I can do. Would it help if I came round?"

I wasn't sure: Jessie is on the pushy side, and I didn't want Suzie stressed, but on the other hand maybe a reminder of her work life might prompt some response. "You can try."

Thursday 2nd October

Jessie rang to say that she visited Suzie this morning. She was up and dressed, but apparently nothing Jessie said made any difference. She tried to pep Suzie up with optimistic talk – "You know how they love you. You'll be right back" – but we all know that in show biz, it's out of sight, out of mind. The hospital says that she'll need to be in this cast, and then a soft one, for about three months, and then there'll be months of physio. All talk of a second series of B&BQs will have to be shelved.

I leave the house early, partly to beat the rush hour, but also because the bank does start at an ungodly hour. Last week I rushed home every night, but I can see that whatever time I get back makes no difference. I just have to make sure I'm there to make – or, realistically, fetch – something for supper. There's a good choice round here – as long as you like curry – and the quality's great. I'm simply not up to cooking, and Suzie's still completely out of it, withdrawn, sometimes making little noises in her throat, but not speaking. Never speaking. Not to me, not to anyone. Last night I stood in the bedroom doorway, wishing I could interpret Suzie's silence, understand what it is she isn't saying. Speak to me, my Suze.

Monday 6th

I can't stand the silence any more. My response to Joe's comment about "too much quiet" came back to me. Little did I know. I've taken to listening to music on headphones as I go round the flat. It won't help anyone if I get depressed too. I'm not good at jollying people along. Suzie is – or was – the sunny one. I wonder whether I should try to contact her father, but I can't imagine that it would help, and besides, I've no idea how to get his address. I don't even know if Suzie has it – and there's no way of finding out.

I feel lost. She is lost. Where's my lovely, loving Suze? I can't deny it, I know that a living part of her has been subsumed into that lifeless bit of fur that lies beside the bed. God knows I've wished it "dead" so many times over the years. Be careful what you wish for.

Wednesday 8th

It's 7:00 p.m. and I'm still at the bank. The fact is I don't want to go home, don't want to confront the silence. I know I have to. I want to support Suzie, care for her. But there's simply no reaction. Nothing I do makes any difference. She barely eats, won't meet my eyes, and above all she still isn't speaking. She's locked in. I wish I knew what she's thinking about in all that silence. When I came home from work last night she wasn't even dressed, still lying on the bed, looking as if she hadn't moved since I left. Looking as if she'd been crying. What was that about? Her hair is straggly, unkempt – this is not the elegant sexy woman that I know. She seems to have lost not only the power of speech but her sense of herself. I looked down on her, my gorgeous girl, a figure as inert as the puppet beside her. I've almost given up talking to her. I don't like the sound of my voice saying the same inane things over and over again. "Hello, Suzie. How are you feeling? Any better? I had a really busy day today,"

The doc says we just have to be patient, that trauma works in mysterious ways. He's referring her to a specialist, but God knows how long that will take, and how much more of this I can take. For goodness' sake, surely it isn't normal to stay mute for so long? There must be more they can do.

I haven't been near the labyrinth – why would I invite more silence into my life? What I'm drawn to is the sound of normal human activity. Not the loud noise of heavy metal or the shouting of drunks but just everyday chat and laughter. And so, strange as it seems, I have begun to look forward to going to the office. At least I'm paying the rent. Despite the misery, that's something to be proud of.

8:00 p.m. I took my time going home, and dropped into the dry cleaners below us before going up to the flat. Abdul is a miserable git, and he suited my mood. Maybe he has reason: I gather that business isn't brisk. Most modern clothes don't need cleaning; they can just be dumped in the washing machine. It's a dying trade. Maybe he could diversify but it isn't his own business and he's made it clear that he isn't paid to think. Anyway, he was willing, as always, to take in a parcel for me when it arrives. I'm expecting something from Amazon, and even if Suzie's up there's no way she will open the door. And now I'd better put the washing on, or she'll have nothing to wear.

Thursday 9th
Nearly a month since the accident. The days are shortening; I've had to put the heating on. I've begun to feel resentful. She doesn't care whether I'm here or not. Is this a silence of indifference or outright hostility? What have I done? What's she punishing me for?

Chapter 14

As I emerged from the horrors of the rush-hour Central Line, I told myself that next time I must mend the puncture. However lacklustre I feel in the morning, however bad the weather, even cycling in fume-ridden London is better than this.

The lift up to the third floor was full of men and a few women in black suits, shaking their umbrellas.

A tall patrician figure unbent enough to address me. "Morning, Orbs." It was one of the partners.

"Oh hi, Simon."

"Good weekend?"

"Yes, fine, thanks (*liar*). How about you?"

"Yes, splendid. My sister's wedding. Got a bit rat-arsed, a bit fragile today." Wry grin, sympathetic laughter from others in the lift. And then Simon spotted a small woman squashed up in the corner. "Oh, good morning, Sonia. How was your holiday?"

Sonia grimaced. "Apart from a four-hour delay at Gatwick and my luggage arriving in Lanzarote, terrific."

"Remind me, where was it you went?"

"Tenerife." Laughter again. "But a nice little villa, pool, sun, caught up on sleep. You know." Grunts of agreement. Yes, they knew.

But when was the last time I had a holiday? Suzie and I have talked about it but, like most of our friends, we're either working so hard there's no time, or we have the time and no money. Sod's law. And we daren't plan too far ahead anyway, because you never know when there might be an opportunity, an audition, a phone call that might make all the difference.

Monday 13th
The office banter is like nectar to my parched soul. However vacuous the chat, at least people are talking to each other. And the usually

confining structures provide a reassuring rhythm in a life that feels like swimming in mud. Bizarrely, I find myself more at home at the bank than ever before. And less at home in our flat. It makes no sense. For the first time the flat feels too small. Normally it's fine – I mean, how many rooms can you be in at the same time? But now it feels as if there's no room to breathe. I love Suzie, of course I do, but we're not used to living on top of each other. I'm used to having a lot of time to myself, to mooching around, just feeling the space around and within me. And, of course, in the present circs I can't do anything about finding real work, work that makes my heart sing.

Naturally we've lost sight of Freddie now. When I have time off from worrying about Suzie, I worry about him. He had been coming on so well, seeing us had all meant so much to him. Will he be feeling abandoned? How is he coping now – will he slither back to being a drug-subdued Mummy's boy?

I've always liked silence. It's an important part of my life. But not one like this – brooding, full of something withheld. At home I now plug myself into my iPod, the radio, anything to remind me that there's a normally functioning world out there. Fooling feels like another country.

Chapter 15

Now that I'm going to the bank more often, however much I keep my head down, I've naturally become more a part of it all, learned more of what's going on, got a little sense of the others. To my surprise, Andrew, the clerk who works in the next office to mine, invited me out for a drink tonight. I was amazed. Why should he bother? He knows nothing about me. All I've done since I've arrived is despise him and the others, and lie to them. I feel ashamed.

So, as he got in the pints, I opened my mouth and tried to begin again. Given the false stories that I've fed them, it's hard to know where to start. And, I have to face it, I know no more of Andrew's life than he does of mine. He is, it turns out, married with three children (he doesn't look old enough), one of whom has Down's syndrome.

"Oh," I said conventionally, "I'm sorry."

Andrew looked a bit affronted. "No need to be sorry," he said. "She's lovely. It's just that her care is a bit more complicated. Annie has given up teaching to spend more time with her."

My turn to open a crack in the armour. I felt on a very vulnerable brink. "My brother," I said, looking at the table, "he has mental health problems." There, it was out, and it was all right. The sky did not fall in. Andrew listened, with sympathy. This is how colleagues are. And it did not mean that I was bound to them hands and feet, man and boy.

And then Miles, one of the other clerks, came into the pub and came over to join us. He gave me a cheery nod. He's a chirpy young man, fresh out of college. "What are you having?" And so began the usual dance.

I envy Andrew and Miles their camaraderie. But then they're full-time and spend a lot of time together. That's the trouble with being part-time and occasional. You never really fit in. But then I've never wanted to,

Andrew crossed his legs. "Ah, but you, Orbs, have another life. I rather envy you. I expect you have lots of different circles of friends."

Do I? Yes, I have a life outside, that's for sure, but friends? The problem is that most of my mates are on the road half the time. We have a close connection when we coincide – part of the same gig, same focus – but there are few people I can just ring for a quick beer and a chinwag.

"By the way," said Miles, well into the second pint, "I've been wondering. I can see that this isn't really your bag. What is it that you really do the rest of the time? Some sort of performing?"

I gaped. Was I that transparent? "What makes you say that?"

"Oh, I dunno. There's a kind of suppressed energy about you, as if you're about to jump up and do something. You have such a mobile face, and a good voice. You'd be great on the stage." Miles paused. "I feel there's more to you than meets the eye. Well, anyway..." He looked away, obviously feeling he'd overstepped the mark.

"I don't use my voice, actually."

"No?"

So then there was nothing for it.

But when I stammeringly tried to explain, I could see that this was a step too far. Their eyes glazed, and there was a shuffle to get in the next round. So they still thought I was weird, but now with more reason!

No one gets fooling. It's not something you can really explain. Just something you are. And as for explaining what Suzie does, not in a million years. They've never met her, and luckily she has a different stage name, so they won't make the connection. And that's the way it's going to stay. I've no idea if they've seen her show or not. I couldn't bear the thought of them ogling her, lusting after her, like most of the men who watched her show. If she ever makes it back on the screen. And then reality kicked in – what chance was there of that?

Mother rang this evening. She always rings in the evening, because she thinks I'm at work all day. I could have done without it: keeping up the chirpy pretence of a normal life. At least I can talk a bit about the bank, because I have actually been going there.

Chapter 16

The one connection I have with my past life – that life of school and family – is my annual trip to Lord's. Because it doesn't start till 11:00 a.m. it's an opportunity, if Suzie is around, for a long and languorous lie-in, maybe breakfast in bed. Not this year, of course. I wasn't sure whether to go or not, but it's something I really look forward to and I knew that, frankly, Suzie was unlikely to notice one way or the other. So I left a note for Rosemary about the leftovers for lunch in the fridge, and arranged breakfast on a tray for when Suzie woke: a nectarine with yoghurt, and a couple of those little round rolls that she likes so much. We usually make do with sliced bread from the corner shop, but I'd picked up the rolls in town in case they might tempt her to eat. Then I put on my glad rags and set off, determined to have a good time.

The walk up from St John's Wood station is part of the day: a parade of mostly men, some with MCC ties and panama hats, many with baskets full of goodies. Nat and Jonathan were already there, waiting for me at the members' entrance. "Morning, Jonners." Yes, we play those silly name games, it's all part of it.

It's Jonathan who organises the day. He's a member of the MCC, and always gets our tickets. Nat brings the champers; both refuse to let me pay. "No," they say every year, "it's our treat." It wouldn't have done to let on that they knew I was hard up – not quite the thing. We don't meet up at other times, and have never met each other's partners, so there's no pressure to tell our stories, whether true or false. It is what it is. Quite a relief. But I'm fond of them both, and I guess they know me pretty well. Not my hidden identity, though having witnessed some of my antics at school they might not have been surprised.

The two of them had been good mates at school, where they

were known as Little and Large. Nat is small and dapper, now with distinguished streaks of grey at his temples. Jon is a bit of a lumbering giant, clumsy and has become a bit of a lush, but he's someone you'd be unwise to underestimate. I knew that his marriage had broken up, and if making money is the only thing you have in your life, it's not surprising if you take to drink.

It feels strange to be part of that gang again – it all seems so far in my past. I always find myself poshing up my accent when I'm with them, reverting to all that schoolboy snobbery. The day is as much about the occasion and meeting my friends as it is about the match. I like cricket, but wouldn't think of going on my own. I've never been to any other ground though I sometimes think that grounds like Headingley or Edgbaston might be more my thing. I really fancy sitting in the party stand dressed up as a banana, a gorilla, Superman or Dame Edna. Sadly, none of my fooling friends are into cricket and I couldn't imagine Nat or Jonners doing any such thing.

But I love the old-fashioned Englishness of the day – what other game stops for tea? – the hats and blazers, and the wit and light-hearted knowledge of the Test Match Special team. Like many in the crowd, I usually listen on headphones when watching. (They can interpret the subtleties and it's not always easy to see the ball.)

At lunchtime we made our way, like hundreds of others, to the Nursery ground, and spread out our picnic on the grass. We don't go in for queuing or overpriced hampers, but bring our own bits and pieces and top up with whatever we fancy during the day.

"So," I asked, "what do you think?"

Nat poured some bubbly into a plastic beaker. "Pretty good, isn't it, though I think Root's a bit late declaring. A bit conservative."

Jonners held out his cup. "We forget how young these chaps are. It's a hell of a responsibility."

"And he's still quite new. Not surprising."

"But, anyway," said Jonners, complacently sipping at his drink, "we can't lose from here."

Nat and I burst out laughing. "Where have I heard that before? England can lose from anywhere. Calypso collapso. You know what they're like."

And more in that familiar vein as we shared our pork pies and cherries and viewed each other with tolerant affection. By mutual consent there was no shop talk. It was just as well: I wouldn't have known what to say. They were both doing very nicely, thank you, and assumed I was doing all right. Neither would have bought the maths teacher story – they knew me too well.

And well enough to notice that I wasn't in a good place.

As we swigged our bubbly, Jonners pressed my arm and said, "Look, old thing, anyone can see something's the matter. 'Fess up. Tell your Uncle Jonners."

Despite his self-mockery, I could see that he really cared. And, come to think of it, it's the self-mockery that makes all the difference. It transforms the appallingly superior world of my parents and school into something altogether warmer and inclusive. That's what makes TMS so delightful. Although the commentators are unbelievably knowledgeable, they don't take themselves too seriously.

"So go on," said Jonners, "Cough it up."

Where to start? "The thing is…it's my Suzie."

They nodded; I'd mentioned her.

"She's ill." Noises of concern. "She hurt her wrist rather badly, but apart from that, apparently there's nothing physically wrong." They looked grave. "But she can't work – and that's everything to her."

Nat looked up from peeling a satsuma. "I've never really known exactly what it is that she does."

"She's in entertainment." That was all I could say. I'd already said too much but was determined not to tell any more lies. I couldn't let on what she did or who she was. It would be our undoing. They didn't press me anyway. My unwillingness to elaborate was pretty obvious. Maybe they thought she was a lap-dancer!

I was a bit the worse for wear when I got home. I should remember that bubbly and beer don't mix, but it's good to let my hair down from time to time. I could see as soon as I walked into the flat that there had been a change. Suzie was almost pleased to see me. I must let her heart grow fonder more often.

Chapter 17

I left the bank early today. I was fed up with the tedium, the pointlessness of staring at a series of noughts – Monopoly money that means nothing. And I felt it was time to make an effort, time I spent more time with my lovely Suzie. On my way home I picked up some (imported) asparagus, one of her favourite things, and thought I'd look online for a recipe of something to go with it.

When I let myself into our flat I was surprised to see Suzie in a long figure-hugging skirt and pottering around in the kitchen, washing up some cups. She turned as I came in, looking, I thought, a little discomfited. I didn't try to touch her.

"Hello, darling. How lovely to see you up and about." She gave me a brief smile and turned away to put the cups in the cupboard. "I've bought some asparagus and thought… " but she had wandered out of the kitchen. I tried to focus on the progress rather than the hurt.

Friday 17th

After Suzie had gone to bed, I sat on my own, my head in my hands, trying not to pour myself a drink. Yes, it was good to see her on her feet, but without a loving embrace, without the customary warmth of her welcome, it felt empty. I'm trying to remember how things were before the accident. Suzie and I used to have such fun. Larking about, being silly. Though, to be frank, that was usually more me than her. Where's the fun in my life now? And where's my fooling?

I must confess I'm hankering after a bit of Joe's wilderness. Getting itchy-footed. Except in childhood I've never stayed so long in one place. If it weren't for Suzie, I'd have been off long ago. So what am I going to do? There's no point in going on like this. My life's a misery and I don't seem to be able to help Suzie. She doesn't even seem to want me in her life. But I can't really think of leaving, can I? How could I abandon her? And, anyway, where would I go? What would I do?

Monday 20th

I've stopped trying to communicate. Nothing I do seems to make any difference. I guess she'll respond when she's ready – if she does. So, although of course I continue to do things for her, look out for her, I've withdrawn. In self-defence, I suppose. I'm trying to live my life – only a half-life maybe, but mine. I tried to make an appointment with our GP – on my own account this time. It would be so good to talk things through with someone, but, apart from the daily emergency surgeries, there are no free appointments until mid-November. No one could call this an emergency, so I've left it. In any case there's probably not much that they could tell me. Patient confidentiality and all that. But I feel very alone. And tense.

Somehow in this imposed silence I've lost my own inner stillness. I'm permanently on edge, straining for a sound, a change, anything.

Tuesday 21st

Work is difficult now in a different way. Now that I have to talk more to the other chaps, I don't know what to say, but after hiding all these months it's impossible not to reveal a bit more.

Suzie had her cast off today. At last. I offered to go with her, but she was mutely adamant about going alone. I sat at my desk, fidgeting with anxiety. It was so hard not to be able to check in with her to find out how it was going. She doesn't even reply to my texts. Why the hell not? She obviously writes to communicate with the doctors and, for all I know, with her friends. Anyway, when I came home this evening, it was to a Suzie in a softer bandage and with a sheet full of exercises. Something seems to have shifted. God, I hope so.

As I cycled home this evening, I overtook Hannah and the children walking slowly down the road. Lali was asleep in her buggy, Subeer enjoying the satisfyingly crunchy noise as he scuffed his wellies through the autumn leaves. A boy after my own heart. I waved and waited for them outside their flat.

When they stopped, Subeer hid behind his mother. Lali is still largely in the eat, sleep and cry phase and I'm not really interested in children until they are old enough to play peek-a-boo, but manners demanded that I peer into the pushchair and comment, "Sweet."

Hannah grinned wryly. "Especially when she's asleep."

As I was talking to his mother, Subeer, who I guess is about five, peeped out from behind her. I winked at him, then paid him no further attention but stood on one leg for the remainder of the conversation, hoping he'd be entertained. Little giggles showed that he was.

I leant my bike against a tree. "Subeer, could you keep an eye on my bike while I help your Mum take the pushchair upstairs?"

When I came down, Subeer was watching my bike with unblinking concentration. I took hold of it.

"Thank you very much, Subeer. Have you got a bike?"

He nodded gravely.

"Is it as big as this one?"

He shook his head.

"Bet it's just as fast, though."

He nodded dubiously.

"How big is it? Is it this big?" – putting my hands about a foot apart.

"No, bigger," he called.

"This big?" holding my hand about a foot from the ground.

"No," he shouted, "much bigger."

"Even bigger than that?" I asked incredulously, then shook my head. "Surely not. Can't be."

Subeer jumped up and down. "It is, it is. Come on, I'll show you."

Hannah laughed from the top of the steps. "Tomorrow, maybe, Subeer. Just now we need to make your tea."

It was good to get to know my neighbours a little better; maybe we'll talk a little more. I carried the bike upstairs, let myself in and braced myself. "Hello, Suzie, I'm home."

Friday 24th
After work today, I walked the Fen Court labyrinth. It was dress-
down Friday at work so there was none of the usual embarrassment
about wearing posh clothes. Seeing the road outside blocked off by the
hoardings of a new building development, ominously blazoned as Fen
Court, I feared at first that my little haven might have succumbed to
corporate ambition, but, as I turned into the little leafy square, I saw
it was still nestling there, holding its own. And so was I. I'd forgotten
that it was the site of a memorial to the abolition of the slave trade:
the poignant sculpture was littered with beer bottles, but the power of
its engravings shone through: a poem with an extraordinary blending
of City terminology and Old Testament language marking the place
of Spirit in this centre of trading: "Cash flow runs deep but spirit
deeper." Dodging the puddles and ignoring curious glances from those
sitting on the benches, I kept the words in my mind as I walked. And
as I made my way home afterwards, there was greater clarity in the air
and sharper outlines of the buildings against the unseasonably blue
sky.

Saturday 25th
Yes, there has been a definite change. Suzie approaches her exercises in
a very determined way, and stays in the sitting room to do them. As I
watch her in the evenings, moving each of her fingers and flexing her
wrist this way and that, I wonder whether she's imagining Bruce back
on her hand, whether she's mentally preparing for the day when she'll
begin again. Though she still doesn't want to be touched, she no longer
avoids my eyes and I'm beginning to hope that she might come back to
me. If it's Bruce that helps her do that, then so be it. I'm not going to
complain. Whatever works.

Tuesday 27th
I know that it's only a little that's changed, but Suzie does look at

me now, and sometimes gives me the hint of a smile. I have no idea how she's been spending her days, but it's true that recently, some six weeks after the accident, she has seemed a bit better, with more energy, less deadness in her eyes. I have hardly dared hope. But I'm making more of an effort to talk again. I'm not good at talking at someone, but I've got to try get some communication going.

My pathetic efforts go something like this: "Hi, Suzie, hope you had a good day? I've had a lot to do. There was so much paperwork to catch up on, I didn't have much time to think. I went out for lunch with one of the assistant managers – Ron's a bit of a bore, but it was good not to eat on my own." (Oh God, does that sound self-pitying?) It feels incredibly artificial – the old Suzie wouldn't be taken in for a moment, but she might appreciate that I'm making the effort.

AN UNFAMILIAR LANDSCAPE

Friday 30th

TGIF. But do I really feel that? One day is much like another. I took a coffee to my desk and opened up the emails. After I'd dealt with the immediate demands, I pulled my inbox towards me, and worked through the papers from my last site visit. I can be quite methodical when I put my mind to it.

It wasn't until the coffee break, when I reached into my bag for my phone, that I noticed something that I didn't remember putting there. It was a small plastic bottle – a bottle for orange juice. But this one was empty, except for a small slip of paper.

I unscrewed the top of the bottle and took the paper out. On one side were written the words: "Hello Orbs", in wobbly handwriting. Suzie's writing. A message from a foreign land. My heart turned over in wonder and delight. My Suzie, managing to be playful even in her desolation. I was electrified, wanted to jump on my bike and pedal home as fast as I could, but I had figures to submit for a meeting in the afternoon. So I went to the gents, shut myself in a cubicle and cried, great sobs of gratitude. I wasn't much use to anybody that afternoon. My head was spinning, my mind all over the place, I did what I had to, then ran away home.

As I cycled back, I hardly noticed the traffic or saw the road; my head was swimming with images of a grand reconciliation and celebration. A feast, in costumes of gold. Maybe I'd dig out our old cardboard crowns. But when I got to the flat, Suzie was asleep. The reality, once again, was emptiness. I sat on the bed and talked to her, told her how much the note had meant to me, hoping that it would in some way reach her, but with no visible effect. And at suppertime I tried to get her to eat something, but she didn't want to know. I heated up a shepherd's pie in the microwave, and, reverting to the slobbish habits of my bachelor days, ate it out of its container. I sat in front of the telly, taking little notice either of what went into my mouth or what passed before my eyes. I tried not to despair. She had sent me a note: I must hang on to that.

Monday 2nd November

It was hard not to believe in my imaginings that everything would fall into place, but of course my fantasies were just that. The weekend passed completely without incident, casting a bleakness that was harder than ever to bear. I kept looking at Suzie, hoping for transformation, but there was nothing to be seen.

Thursday 5th

Being at work is even tougher now that I've had a glimpse of the real Suzie. I really struggled today and cycled back, feeling quite despondent and unmoved by the occasional bangs and rockets shooting up into the sky. Guy Fawkes. So what?

But when I got home, feeling harassed and weary, there was my lovely girl in the hallway, her hair gleaming, and dressed in that lovely shimmering green thing that she knows I love. She stood there a bit tentatively, and said with a little voice husky from disuse, "Hello, Orbs. How was your day?"

I stood there, bike helmet in hand, dripping with sweat and trying not to cry.

"Suze? Oh, my darling." I dropped my helmet and gently gathered her like a fragile flower in my arms, my head in her hair, breathing in her fragrance. "My day? It's wonderful."

Of course it was all too soon, but I couldn't help blurting out: "Darling Suze, would you like to go out tonight? It's bonfire night. We could go and watch the fireworks?" She shook her head, but leaned into me in the first show of affection she had given me since it all happened. My cup ran over, and so, in the end, did my eyes.

We lay beside each other that night, holding hands, she sleeping, and I awake and hardly daring to breathe.

Chapter 18

For the next couple of weeks I watched anxiously over Suzie, to see if she showed signs of sinking back into that soundless stupor. I still didn't understand. Had the silence overwhelmed her, or had she in some sense chosen to be silent because the reality of a world without Bruce was too terrible to bear? I didn't dare ask, for fear of what I might hear. And after what she'd been through, I didn't want to disturb her fragile peace. I made an effort to carry on much as before, wanting to allow her the space and time to come back into herself.

But as the days went by, I relaxed my anxiety. In my diary I wrote, *It seems as if we are indeed over that awful period in our lives; she is recovering, and we are coming through.* A week or so after the awakening, I woke with joy in my heart, looked down at the still sleeping form of my beloved and nipped out to get some croissants. I made coffee and took it back to bed.

Suzie stirred lazily, a sight that made me stir too. God, I was horny.

"Hello, Orbs, that's nice. Shouldn't you be at work?"

"I'm taking the day off. Time I did anyway. It's so wonderful you're recovered, darling. Let's do something to celebrate. What about the seaside?"

Suzie looked uncomfortable.

"What's the matter?"

"I can't today. I've got something on."

"What?"

"Someone's coming round."

My green antennae were immediately alerted. "Oh, who?"

Suzie looked even more uncomfortable. One of the things I've always loved about her is her inability to lie. "Er, Freddie."

"Freddie?"

Suzie saw my look, sat up, and put her hand on mine. "Don't

be silly, Orbs. As if I would! And anyway, it's not me Freddie's interested in. It's Bruce."

Although I knew that was probably the truth, I was so incensed that nothing could appease me. It turned out that Freddie had been coming round most days he was in London, that Suzie had somehow been able to communicate. How? With Bruce out of the picture I couldn't imagine. I didn't ask. I didn't (and passionately did) want to know. Despite all my efforts, all that I'd been through with her since the accident, all that Suzie and I mean to each other – or I thought we did – it hadn't been me that had wrought this transformation – it had been *Freddie*. I left the room, threw some clothes on, and slammed out of the house. I didn't care where I went.

The trouble was I had no one to confide in. No one knew what was going on. Strangely, it's something that Dad might have understood, but he's so deaf now that it would have been hopeless to try. Not exactly something I could shout about down the phone. I knew Jonners was away, so in the end I rang Nat, arranged to meet for a drink that evening, and went to work after all.

Chapter 19

After that, Freddie didn't come round for a while. At least Suzie said he didn't, and I had to make myself believe her. We didn't discuss it, but I guess Suzie must have warned him off. I certainly had no wish to see him. I was furious. Not sure I'd ever wanted to see him – I had never been part of that cosy little triangle anyway. I know he's been through a tough time and all that, and I do care about him – he's my brother, after all – but it still felt like a betrayal: creeping round behind my back.

So I was guarded when a week or so later he rang.

"Hello, Freddie." I knew better than to ask how he was and there was nothing else I wanted to ask him. He was a bit taken aback by my tone, but he couldn't contain himself. There was a barely suppressed excitement in his voice as he said, "I'm ringing to give you some news."

"Oh?" What news could he possibly have that would interest me?

"I'm afraid I won't be visiting for a bit. The fact is, I've got a job."

Jaw-dropping. "A job?" My brother?

Apparently, the plant nursery where he'd been doing a few hours a week had taken a shine to him and had offered him a full-time maternity leave replacement.

"There's even the possibility of getting some day release to study horticulture. I rang to say thank you. If it hadn't been for the three of you (!), I would never have got this far. You really helped me get back on my feet."

"Well." I swallowed and ground out, "Thank you. I'm very glad." Why do family always make me feel bad?

"Maybe I'll make enough to leave Mum and Dad's."

Yes, well, one step at a time, Freddie.

But my anger was mostly directed at Suzie. She hadn't

actually lied – she doesn't – but she hadn't told me either. Well, I guess she wasn't speaking at the time, but there are ways... I did blame her, and made that clear.

Tuesday 24th
The flat is no longer silent, but we aren't back to normal – whatever that is – and it comforts me to take refuge here. I try to make allowances but I'm still pretty raw. I so needed to believe that I'd been the one to awaken my Beauty.

Suzie doesn't talk as readily as she used to. As if the period of silence has purged her of excess, she seems to be picking her words with care. She is also a less reliably sunny character these days. I'm having to get used to a new partner. Not the soft, ever-accepting woman I've been living with for two years, but someone less accommodating. Sometimes she's quite sharp with me. I suppose it's more real, but there are times, astonishingly, when I wish Bruce was back in our lives. Of course, I know that, deep down, she's always been a tough cookie. After all, even if she's used Bruce to do it, she's used to pinning politicians down, holding them to account.

Now that Suzie has regained the power of speech, the GP has offered her CBT, a therapy to talk things through, but she and I both knew the source of the trauma. She's grieving. She doesn't need to talk it through with strangers. It might help her, but having kept Belinda secret for so long, she isn't likely to break the habit now.

But what about me?

Wednesday 25th
I still wonder what I'm doing. For want of anything better, I continue to plod back and forth to the bank in a new smart suit, as to the manner born. I've became part of the institution. Now that I'm more reliably in the office I'm used more often for site visits. Today I went with Ron, the assistant manager, to a new client in Hampstead. In the cab, Ron briefed me, then said, "This is what we really need you for, Orbs." After fifteen minutes or so of polite engagement, Ron left me to collect

the nitty-gritty. Then back to the office (by public transport, natch) to input the information. Dreary, dreary work.

But I'm so grateful for my colleagues. Despite how I've behaved, people are kind and once a week I now go with some of them for a couple of beers at the local, where they're all pretty well known. But I'm not one of them, and we all know it. No one asks about the maths teaching – I'm not sure they've ever believed it. The work is as mindless as ever, and now Mondays descend each week with a foggy predictability. Something that started as a little sideline to earn the occasional bit of pocket money has become a JOB, with obligations. Where's my world? The random world in which I can wander and breathe?

There's no chance of moving to a different flat now; it's hard enough to pay the rent as it is. I suppose there's a certain satisfaction in paying the bills, not relying on Suzie. But it's not how I see myself. Is this my role, my contribution now? A contribution from a false identity. The walls are closing in.

Chapter 20

It was late, and we were sprawled on the settee after supper. I'd done the washing-up as usual – it's not a job for the one-handed – but Suzie had insisted on making the coffee. I couldn't bear to see her struggle, so had left her to it. As she pottered in the kitchen, I texted a colleague about arrangements for the following day.

When I closed my phone and looked up, the coffee was on the table and Suzie was gazing out of the window.

"Thanks, Suze."

She didn't answer, and fear caught at my throat.

"Suze?"

She shook herself and turned to focus on me. "Sorry, I was miles away."

That's what I was afraid of. "Are you okay?"

"Yes, I'm fine."

I must be patient. It's going to take time.

As Suzie's recovery continued, and she was well enough to take herself off to her weekly physio session and, with her one good hand, take on some of the household tasks, I watched her progress with some nervousness. It was hard to know how things stood between us. As she continued to stretch her fingers and rotate her wrist, she showed no sign of taking Bruce up again. The inert bundle of material still lay on the bedside table on her side of the bed, untouched. I found myself feeling sorry for him. And wondered when and whether Suzie would find again her purpose in life.

She seemed to have little idea of time, needed to be prompted to get up and go to bed, and was surprised when mealtimes came and went. It was as if she had been pulled out of a deep place in the earth; indeed, in bed one night, under the cover of darkness, she confided that it was with the greatest difficulty that she had emerged from wherever she had been. We were lying on our backs in the dark, hand in hand, staring up at the ceiling. Suzie moved her head to rest it on my shoulder.

"You've no idea what it was like, Orbs. I thought the world had come to an end – in fact, I wanted it to. I'd lost everything. I was so scared at the beginning – and so guilty."

"*Guilty?*"

"Yes. All the trouble I was causing, letting everyone down."

"I thought you were blaming me."

"You? What on earth for?"

"I don't know. That's just how it felt."

"You see...I had reason to feel guilty."

I put my arm under her neck and pulled her to me. "Nonsense."

"Anyway, then, strangely, I got horribly used to it and in the end it was hard to come out. It was a dark place, but surprisingly seductive. I wanted to be left alone. The silence was so comforting."

"*Comforting?*"

"Yes, wrapped up in my own little world. Nothing could get at me. I suppose I understand better what you get from the silence of your world...the fooling, the labyrinths."

Wow.

"In fact –"

"Yes?"

"If it hadn't been for you, I might have stayed there. I don't know where I would have been without you."

"Without Freddie, you mean."

"Nonsense, Orbs. He just showed me how lucky I am."

And then, almost chastely, we kissed.

Chapter 21

It's always been my favourite time of day, preparing supper together. In the old days, it was a time when Bruce was laid aside, and now, Suzie with her one hand and I with my two were once again working alongside each other, chopping, frying and stirring. It felt good, a wind-down from the preoccupations of the day.

I was content. Suzie chuntered on about her progress with the physio, what she'd found in the market, the closure of our favourite bakers. Everyday things. To be frank, I listened more to the sound of her voice than the content. It didn't really matter what she said. It was just so lovely to hear her voice again.

"Orbs?"

"Sorry. What did you say?"

"Really, Orbs, sometimes I think you should have been a monk."

A monk? She can't have meant celibate. I visualised myself with a tonsure, in a brown robe – is that Franciscan? Yes, I rather fancy that. And didn't St Francis consider himself a fool? Must look it up. One problem: I don't believe in God. What kind of God would I believe in, if I were a monk? God as a fool, a trickster? I remembered how that morning my dressing gown had caught the loo paper and it had unrolled to the floor. I laughed at the time and now as I remembered it, I laughed again. God as trickster. We could have fun together.

But on reflection I'd rather be a hermit. Don't fancy having to put up with all those other men.

"Orbs, are you listening?"

"Sorry." I brought myself back to the present.

"Honestly, you're impossible."

I know, but it's quite a nice place to be!

I turned down the gas and tried to dredge up something of

interest to say. "What about your column? How's it going this month?"

"Oh, I'm so slow typing with one hand, I decided to plead illness and give it a miss. Especially as all those engineering works make getting anywhere so tiresome. Luckily, I did quite a few in advance, so there are plenty of columns in reserve. Anyway, if he's desperate, I'm sure George can find something else to fill the space."

She wiped her hands on the towel. "Orbs, tell me something. Freddie told me that your parents think I'm shy. Why would they think that?"

I squirmed. "Well, you do like to keep your – and our – private life, well, private, don't you?"

Suzie picked up an aubergine and continued chopping. "Don't mislead people, Orbs, especially about me."

"No, Suze, you're right. I just wanted to protect us. I know how Mother would cross-examine you. I'm sorry."

And so the days went by, both of us feeling our way through an unfamiliar landscape. I didn't know what to expect from Suzie, and my own moods were rather erratic. I tried to keep going, but there was an underlying restlessness which sometimes caught me unawares.

* * *

"Orbs, I want to talk to you."

When Suzie came out of the bedroom, I'd just finished my morning exercises and was sitting sweatily on the floor. "Oh, Suze, can we save it for another time? I'm dying for a shower."

"We never find another time."

I ran my hands through my hair and sighed. "Okay, go on."

Suzie sat on the arm of the settee, and swung her legs. "These past few weeks…"

"Yes?"

"Be patient. This is hard for me. You know all those times recently when you begged me, 'Speak to me, Suze'." So she had heard me. "You have no idea how often in the past I've wanted to say to you, 'Speak to me, Orbs'."

I was startled, and a bit defensive. "Well, I'm not a chatty person."

"No, but am I supposed to be a mind reader? In fact, I've been thinking. I've had a lot of time to think – no" – she put up her hand to stop any sympathetic response – "let me speak. It occurred to me how little we speak about anything that matters. The way we've lived. We've been so often in different places. You were asleep when I came in, and I was asleep when you went out. Even when we were in the same place, you were usually tapping away on your laptop or locked into that unfathomable silence of yours. Bruce knew more about me than you do."

I was floored not only by what she was saying but by the fact that she had put Bruce in the past tense.

I'd had no idea. I seem to have had no idea about anything much.

"Without Bruce, there's only you to talk to."

Oh, thanks.

Seeing my look, she said, "Well, you know what I mean. There's a gap."

And it was true. Suzie is leaning on me more these days. She needs more from me. I've had to encourage her to go out and about. It's hard for her, she's lost so much confidence and worries that she'll be spotted, challenged, by someone on the street. But as we gently go about our old routines: to the butcher, the corner shop, the market, she's begun to relax.

* * *

This evening Suzie was unusually quiet. There was a book on her lap, but she wasn't reading it.

I looked up from my computer. "Are you all right?"

"Not really."

"What's wrong?"

"I don't know where I am."

"What do you mean?"

"I've come back into a world where nothing seems the same."

I went over to her and stroked her shoulder. "Don't worry, darling. Your arm is getting stronger all the time. You'll soon have Bruce back. I know it will take –"

Suzie shook her head violently. "No, no, you don't understand. The connection is broken. I won't start again."

I just looked at her. I didn't take her seriously. I couldn't imagine it.

"I've had plenty of time to think...and to grieve. I know it's over. That's why I feel lost. I've no idea what to do."

"There's your column."

"Yes, but that's not enough."

I didn't know what to say.

So I was glad when George emailed Suzie to warn her they were running out of material. It meant she had to focus, so she took a deep breath and began to plan some trips for Vox Pop. For her first trip, to Bristol, I went with her to Paddington, waving her off on the train. She'll be all right, my Suze. At heart she's strong.

But I hope I'm up to it. I must say it's all a bit knackering. Not sure about this talking lark. Some things are better unsaid.

Chapter 22

A few days later, as I got into bed, I noticed that Bruce was no longer on the bedside table. I'd simply got out of the way of noticing him. How long had he been gone? Had Suzie taken him to Bristol? But when she came back, there was still no sign. I hesitated to mention it, though if Suzie had taken him up again it was a sign of recovery. I watched for a day or two, then I did bring it up. Suzie was in her dressing gown, her laptop on the table in front of her.

I stood in front of her. "Suze, where's Bruce? I haven't seen him for a while."

She didn't look up. "Oh, I gave him to Freddie."

I was thunderstruck. Gave away her beloved companion, the tool of her trade? My shock must have shown, but Suzie continued to look at her screen, saying in a matter-of-fact tone, "Yes, I can't see I'll be working with him again, and he means so much to Freddie. I'm glad he's gone to a good home."

"But..."

She shut her computer with a sigh, and looked at me. "No, Orbs, please don't say anything. I don't want to talk about it. Of course it's painful, but I feel that that phase of my life is over. I've had a lot of time to think about it. It's time I moved on."

To what?

"And, anyway, Freddie... Freddie..." She leaned back and sighed more deeply, in a way that reminded me of my mother. "He really needs Bruce. I really think Bruce can help him. You know, Freddie was telling me that it was so good belonging to that network for hearing voices. Some of the others say that they have voices talking about them – horrid, whispering, plotting voices. He feels good that his are nothing like that. His all speak *to* him – and he's begun to see them as part of himself. So Bruce can be a vehicle for that. D'you see?"

I only knew that she had been seeing my brother again without telling me, that Freddie seemed to occupy a lot of her attention. That she had given her beloved puppet to Freddie, and without asking or even telling me. Not that I would have wanted the dratted creature. She knew I'd have thrown him in the bin. But never mind that. All I could think of was that there was more to her relationship with Freddie than she was telling me. He's always been bad news. Why the hell had I allowed him back into my life?

I couldn't bear to be in the flat. After all I'd been through with and for her. I flung out of the door and hurtled down the steps. To hell with our leisurely Sunday lunch. As a gesture of protest, I went to the corner shop and bought a particularly meaty and, as it turned out, rather disgusting sandwich. The assistant was on his phone and took my money without a word. Although I wasn't dressed for the cold wind that hit me, I turned up my collar and went to the park anyway. I stomped down the paths until I beat the fury from my blood and the chill from my bones.

It was, as always, sobering and good to be among the majesty and sanity of trees. I've never thought that hugging a tree is stupid. I'd like to think that I can learn from the fortitude of an oak, and soak up some of its deep-rooted, long-lived sap. Eventually I calmed down and tried to put Freddie out of my mind, tried to absorb the enormity of what Suzie had just told me. I sat on a rain-spattered bench and considered what it meant. This could change everything.

I tried to keep my cool as I walked up the stairs to our flat. I poured myself a beer and went in search of Suzie, who had been washing her hair. From the fragrant smells that greeted me, it seemed that she had gone ahead with the meal we had planned.

I knocked on the bathroom door. "Suzie, can we talk?"

"Sure." She rubbed her hair with the towel in a vigorous, rather defiant way and followed me into the sitting room. She obviously wasn't going to apologise.

I took a deep breath. "Suze, I can't believe what you just told me. Do you mean you're giving up the vent?"

"Uh-huh."

"But that's unthinkable. It would be such a waste. Just as you're making a real name for yourself. You have such a talent. You are so loved."

"Maybe I want to be loved in a different way."

What did that mean?

"But, Suze, what will you do?"

She turned back into the bathroom and called over her shoulder, "Don't worry, Orbs, I'll think of something."

But I did worry. Was she really so unconcerned? I couldn't believe it. After all these years. It's been her *life*. It felt cataclysmic. At least one of us had been following our dream (as well as paying the bills). Was I stuck at the bank forever? It hadn't occurred to me that my freedom to fool was reliant on Suzie's work. It wasn't a comfortable thought.

Her agent, of course, was devastated. The career that she had nurtured was down the drain. When the news broke, she rang me in desperation – not something she's given to doing.

"Orbs, is that you?"

"Hi, Jessie, yes."

"Can you talk?"

"Yes." Suzie was asleep.

"The thing is," Jessie said, "I don't know what to do. I talked to Suzie yesterday, and she told me what she'd done."

"Yes, she said."

"God knows, the accident was bad enough. Cancelling the series was almost the beginning of the end. But we've managed to pull it back a little. There's still a bit of interest – we can play the compassion card, even turn the mystery of her disappearance to our own advantage. But getting rid of Bruce is a complete disaster. What are we going to do?"

We? I wasn't sure our interests were identical but I could

imagine her anxiety. I just couldn't think of anything to say. I was finding it hard enough to cope with all the shocks and changes in my life without considering anyone else's.

Chapter 23

Saturday is market day. Actually, any day is market day, because Chrisp Street is open most of the time. But Saturday morning is when we usually go – especially when I'm working at the bank. When we're both around, it's something we enjoy doing together, especially on a crisp winter day though, as we're not early risers, it can get a bit crowded, full of largely black-clothed women, and children getting under everyone's feet. Although today, for some reason, it was depleted, we still enjoyed wandering around. It's a big market edged by shops and much of it under cover. Among the kitchen equipment, ironmongery and textiles are stalls displaying an array of mellow fruitfulness, including a variety of green objects of different shapes and sizes – large and shiny, smaller crinkly ovals and snake-like strings of green beans half a metre long. We're not that adventurous: we wouldn't know what do with half of them. Maybe we should ask Hannah to come with us some time and tell us what's what. I must say it's good to be able to handle the produce – like European women, people round here expect to know what they're getting.

As we walked back, with a bag in Suzie's good hand and a rucksack on my back, we discussed what we might cook for the weekend. How good it was to breathe a little, to taste a little leisure. But a little was what there would be. The shadow of Monday was already upon me. I groaned.

"Just two days before it all starts again. The thought appals me."

Suzie squeezed my arm. "Just don't think about it. Let's enjoy the weekend."

As we went up the stairs to our flat, she said, "Orbs, I've been wondering. What have you told them at work?"

"Told them?"

"About us, about what else you do."

As I got out the keys, I felt a decided chill in the air. "Well, nothing much. I've mentioned you, of course."

"And the days you're not at the bank?" I could feel her stillness behind me.

Oh God. No lies, I had promised myself. I opened the door and, still not facing her, took the rucksack off my back. "I...I told them I taught maths."

"Maths."

"Yes."

"You lied."

"Well – "

"You lied. You lied to your parents about me, and to your colleagues about what you do."

"Suzie –" I turned and reached out for her, but she shook me off, her eyes blazing.

"Why do men lie? Do you know how my father lied? Do you know that it wasn't until I was fifteen that I heard from my cousin how my mother died? Not in a car crash, as my father had always told me, but by drowning in her lover's swimming pool. And then he lied about the next woman in his life, pretended they hadn't met till after Mum's death. And now we don't speak, so I don't have to listen to any more of his lies."

I didn't know. I had had no idea. "Why didn't you tell me?"

"Why? What difference would it have made? I thought you were different. All that stuff about *being true*." These last two words, spat out with such scathing disdain, robbed me of my breath.

And there we stood, in the hall in our coats, staring at each other.

Chapter 24

The weekend was hardly the delight I had hoped for. We spent most of it apart, catching up with our messages and our friends, and the food we'd bought stayed mostly in the fridge, each of us snacking separately on convenience foods. It took us until Sunday evening to get over our spat. Maybe because Monday was looming, I felt the need to put things in perspective. Suzie had been through a traumatic time; she was still in recovery, and that story of her father was truly shocking. And she was right. I hadn't been truthful; I had to do something about it.

I went into the bedroom where Suzie was lying on the bed, a book beside her, staring at the ceiling.

I sat down on the bed beside her. "Suze, I'm sorry I've been such an idiot. I guess I was just trying to protect us."

She gave a little grunt of acknowledgement, but didn't reply. What more could I say? It was hard to apologise and it wasn't all my fault anyway. She could have been more gracious. I went into the other room, opened up my computer, and tried to find some light relief.

As the working week rolled on, things calmed down. The bank was its boring and predictable self, and for once no new domestic dramas erupted to undermine our fragile peace. We were on an even-ish keel.

* * *

Suzie and I had resumed our lovemaking but my unsureness about – well – everything made me tentative. Loving, yes, but ineffectual. Suzie's gentleness with my failure that night was just too much. I rolled away from her and buried my face in the pillow.

Suzie spooned round my back and put her arms around me.

"Sweetheart, don't. It's all right, really. It doesn't matter. It'll come right."

"I – I just don't know."

"Don't know what?"

"Anything. What to do. Where we are. How we will go on." Now there was no blaming Bruce, or Suzie's busyness. The emptiness was plain to see. I'd never known Suzie without Bruce. Though I'd got a little of my Suze back, there was still something missing. I hated to admit it, but I wasn't used to Bruce not being there. To some extent he let me off the hook. He'd been a presence in our little household, and Suzie was not the same without him. First Bruce, then Freddie, never me.

And now the only thing I'd been able to contribute to our lives had failed. Maybe I couldn't cope with her full attention. What kind of man was I?

I didn't sleep much, and early the next morning I left Suzie asleep, snatched a coffee, threw on some clothes and, taking with me nothing but my front door key, walked out into the street. It was overcast: a dull and featureless morning, with not even a cat to be seen. I wasn't aiming to get anywhere but unsurprisingly found myself in the cemetery. Best place for me. There was no one about at that time of day, and it was a bit spooky. I'm not wild about wandering around alone in deserted places though I can take care of myself. I look scrawny but I keep my eyes open and I'm actually pretty fit. You have to be in our business.

And then, naturally enough, I found myself at the Chalk Maze. I hadn't been there in a long time. Somehow, during the painful weeks of Suzie's silence, I hadn't been able to bring myself to go there. There'd been enough silence at home.

But now I could try. It might help. I wasn't in costume, hadn't brought my nose, but without phone or watch I mentally tried to bring myself into that state, opening myself to the newness of the moment. At the labyrinth, I took off my shoes and socks and stood on the ground.

Walking the labyrinth is like coming home. Why had I likened what I find here to the deadness of the flat? This is no silent emptiness, but a place full of natural sounds, like the noise of the wind in the trees. I read somewhere that because the leaves of trees are different shapes and sizes, every tree responds to the wind with its own unique sound. The silence here is not only punctuated by the sounds of everyday life, it also has its own presence. Or if not a presence, at least a sense of fertile potential.

The setting of the labyrinth is a strange combination of high-rise flats in one direction and in the other nothing but trees. With the clatter of trains and container lorries no one could call this place peaceful. There are, of course, labyrinths in beautiful rural surroundings – walking one in the middle of nowhere, open to the elements, can be a delight. But the two that I walk regularly, surrounded as they are by urban noise and grime, have a particular gritty reality. This is how I live, after all. Peace in the hubbub, space in confusion, a desert in the city.

The last time I'd walked the Chalk Maze had been in the height of summer, but the labyrinth now was a bare and starker place, and my slow and mindful walk was on fallen leaves made crunchy by the frost. Instead of butterflies and a profusion of flowers, the maze was bordered by the occasional clump of grass and guarded by dry spear-like plants, some six-foot tall. Paying attention to the occasional sharp stone and with the cool unevenness of the ground under my feet – heel, sole, toes, I walked on a path that wound, as always, back and forth, in a clockwise, then anti-clockwise direction. I stayed quite a while in the time-free zone of the centre and then came out, walking slowly, meditatively, allowing my mind to float.

And when I arrived home, much later than I'd thought, I hope I brought a little of that stillness with me. Suzie was in the sitting room, prattling to Rosemary on the phone, her long legs looped over the arm of the chair. By the sound of it, the conversation was likely to last for a while. My Suze back in gear. All was right with the world.

But of course there's an elephant – or, rather, a fox – in the room. We don't talk about Bruce but even in his absence he lies between us. I can't imagine how Suzie feels without him, after all these years. I worry that she'll regret getting rid of him and throwing away her whole career. Maybe a sense of freedom will come later. For now, I'm sure she's in mourning.

So, no more Belinda. (Well, I guess she might re-emerge, but I think it unlikely. The public are quick to forget; they don't like gaps.) So begins a new phase in our lives – a life almost in the open. Not completely, because Vox Pop is still anonymous, but people in the trade know who writes it. And as for me, I no longer have to tell lies at the bank. They know I do something "in entertainment", but really don't care about the details. I can't say this more exposed life is always comfortable; it's scary, makes me feel vulnerable. But at least it's more of a piece, and I don't have to remember which version of the truth I've told to whom.

Suzie's soft bandage came off a few days ago but she is obediently continuing with her exercises. Her arm looks thinner – I don't know if it is, but it's certainly naked now, unadorned, strangely vulnerable. No bandage, no puppet. I'll have to get used to that. She is as beautiful as ever, but pale and a bit pinched. It's been a tough time but I feel we're getting through it.

Suzie's future is constantly in my mind, and I worry about how on earth to mention it. She's so touchy these days. It never seems to be the right time. There are possibilities, I know – you can even do vent acts on radio – there were examples way back, like Educating Archie *– but I don't know how Suzie would take to that, and you'd miss her wonderfully visual charisma. And ratings (and pay) would be nothing like the same. Maybe a better idea would be those puppets that sit on a false arm – but that would mean Suzie having to learn something new all over again.*

The thing is, there's never been a time when it's been just her and me and, to be frank, although I'm thrilled to bits to be rid of Bruce and, to some extent, Freddie, I'm scared of the emptiness. How will we cope on our own?

It's only now that it's all stopped that I realise how much damage being a vent has done to Suzie. Of course, the accident and then the isolation have knocked her confidence, but it's not just that. Without Bruce, she's not the same. All those years of sharing herself with an inanimate object have taken their toll. Maybe the public perception of ventriloquism isn't so far from the truth.

A NEW VOICE

Chapter 25

When I came in from work, Suzie was laying the table. We had a hug. "Supper in ten minutes, okay?"

"Yes, fine. Sorry I'm a bit late. I went for a swim." As I went upstairs to get out of my suit, Suzie called up to me. "Oh, Orbs, I've got some news."

"Oh yes?" I turned.

"Yes." How pretty she looked in her silly little pinny. "A publisher contacted me. Profile, I think they're called. "They want to meet. They think my Vox Pop columns might make a book – a sort of oral history. The Brits as we are now."

I ran downstairs and put my hands on her shoulders. "But that's terrific. Good for you, Suze."

"I've had a word with George, and he's all for it. Of course it won't have my name on it, and it's not my copyright, but I'll get a hefty fee."

"Wonderful."

"Yes," she said with her old dazzling smile, "I must say I'm pleased."

* * *

The book deal seems to have energised Suzie. She's got back a lot of her drive and determination, and after a battery of phone calls, she's taken herself off to the Midlands to research her column.

While she was away, I did some thinking. As I settled down into a quieter time, the vibrations of my labyrinth walk stirred in me and after a few days, I realised I'd brought something other than a more peaceful state out with me – an understanding that this was not just about me. The fooling, the joy, the stillness.

It's at moments like that that I let go of the voice in my head – unlike Freddie, I don't have many voices, just one – the voice that asks me what I'm doing with my life. "What do you do all day? Seems to me you're just wasting time."

As Eamon, my painter friend, says, "It's hard to persuade anyone (or yourself) that you're doing anything when you're observing, or thinking. No one pays you for thinking." And, unlike Eamon, I don't even have anything tangible to show at the end of it. When I'm at the bank or on a gig, I can convince myself that I'm doing something, whether useful or not. Of course, there are the household things to do – Suzie and I have always shared them. But, still, I don't have a real job. My poor hardworking parents who imagine that at least one of their sons is making something of himself. They did their best to instil into us the puritan work ethic. I never really bought into it, but I live with the shadow of guilt.

I don't kid myself that all my "being" time is productive. "Sometimes I sits and thinks, and sometimes I just sits." Where does my increased awareness get me? Or, more to the point, where does it get anyone else? How does it contribute to the world? Brings joy, sometimes, yes, but I really admire Lucy, Joan and Chuck who bring out the foolish joy in sick children and dementia patients. They have a purpose, but nothing like that has really spoken to me. And there's no point pretending – it simply wouldn't work.

When I think back to the great fools, the Shakespearean ones, I realise that they were using their wisdom to engage with the issues of the day. And activist fools still exist. I once saw a wonderful video of a group of clowns in the States, who turned up at a demonstration of the Ku Klux Klan and whose white-faced response to the red-faced fury of the separatists was ridicule. The clowns met the KKK's shouts of "white power, white power" with prepared cut-out letters and props: "White flour?" they called, and threw the flour up in the air.

"White power, white power!"

"White flower?" Throwing white flowers into the air.

The KKK were incensed, screaming: "WHITE POWER, WHITE POWER!"

"Ah, we've got it. Wife power." And the women clowns lifted up the men.

Yes, I know they are clowns but I can forgive them their white faces. They have the power of fools.

* * *

I was glad to see Suzie back. There's only so much time that I can spend thinking. I carried her case upstairs and sat on the bed as she unpacked. Packing, unpacking. It's second nature to us both. As she had only been on Suzie jobs, she'd been able to travel light; Belinda gear took more room.

"How was the trip?"

"Ooh, tiring. But good. I talked to some school kids about how they feel about exams, and to some people on a retirement course – planning what they'll do. I've got some really good material. Some people are scared – just have no idea of what they're going to do with themselves. Others are really looking forward to having more time to spend on other things. I love the fact that people are so different. And have such different expectations. I talked to the wife of a long-haul airline pilot. They retire early, and apparently BA runs retirement courses to help couples deal with it. Isn't that splendid?"

"Mmm, yes, it is. You know, Suze, you're so good at what you do."

"Well, I really like it. But, as I said before, it's not enough. There's a big hole."

"Could you go back to reporting?"

"No, done that. I need something new to get my teeth into."

I could see that. Humouring her, I said, "You could always go into politics."

Suzie opened the wardrobe to hang up her suits. "No, Orbs. I'm not a politician."

"That's your strength. No one trusts them anymore. Haven't you noticed? It's the non-politicians who are getting into power."

She considered. "But they'd never take me seriously."

It had been a casual suggestion, the idea coming out of nowhere, but I was warming to it now.

"They know that you get the truth out of people. They'll trust you."

"You think?" She walked about the room, pondering. "It's an interesting idea, Orbs. But I'm not a party political person."

"Stand as an independent, then. Crowdfund it. I bet you'll get a lot of people supporting you, especially if you stand on a no lies, anti-corruption ticket. Like Martin Bell, the man in the white suit. Remember him?"

I'm not sure she did but I could see that the idea had taken hold.

"What about that Tory who's being done for sexual harassment?" I remembered too late that he was to have been one of her victims on B&BQs. Her silence confirmed that it had not been a happy choice.

After a pause, she said, "I think UKIP came second there. Not much chance of getting a radical agenda through."

"Or fight a hard Brexiteer in a constituency that voted Remain. Lots of possibilities. You have so many contacts. I'm sure you can make it. What about Geoff? He's pretty influential – look how he got that TV series for you – and he thinks a lot of you."

"He also wants to get into my knickers. I don't want to encourage him."

My jaw dropped. I remembered how he had watched her at the party, but then so had a lot of men in the room. "You never said."

"No, but then there were a lot of things I never said."

Quite. But now I worried what else might come out of the woodwork. "Is there anyone else I should know about?"

"Nobody significant." She grinned mischievously and squeezed my arm, "Don't worry, darling. I can look after myself." She stretched. "Oof, I'm tired. Thanks for that, Orbs. It's given me food for thought. Even if I don't feel up to it."

"Come on, Suzie, be daring. You have such a reputation. People know who you are and –"

Suzie stared. "Know who I am? What do you mean? Nobody knows who I am."

"Well…"

"Oh, I've got it now. It's B&BQs that you think will persuade people. Are you suggesting I go public about Belinda? After all this time? You know how important being anonymous is to me. Having managed to keep it quiet for all these years, why would I reveal it now? And" – her voice rose – "of course if I don't tell people, I'd have no special pull. So that's that, then. Forget it."

Trying not to cry, she closed the empty case with a snap, reached up to put it back on top of the wardrobe, and ran from the room.

She was right, of course. But what a disappointment. I had begun to get excited.

Chapter 26

I picked my moment. I'd been thinking about it all day at work, shopped in my lunch hour and made a point of leaving early. At home, I banished Suzie from the kitchen and spent an hour or so preparing a platter of steam-cooked vegetables with a home-made aioli sauce. I adorned the plate with flowers, put a candle on the table and, feeling rather proud of myself, folded the napkins into flower shapes. Belgian truffle chocolates for afters. In producing this rather fine meal, maybe I wasn't being very subtle. Certainly Suzie smelled a rat. After suitably complimentary remarks, as we carried the dishes back to the kitchen, she called over her shoulder:

"So, what was all that in aid of, Orbs?"

"What do you mean? You know how I love treating you. Aren't I allowed to do that anymore?"

"And?"

I sighed. "Yes, all right. There is also something I want to say. Could we sit down?"

Suzie gave me what I think is called an old-fashioned look, but then poured herself a glass of water and went back into the sitting room.

We sat on the settee, facing each other and leaning against the arms at either end. I looked my lover in the face and braced myself. "Please don't take this the wrong way, but don't you – don't you think you might be rather overdoing the secrecy? Think about it. Vox Pop, B&BQs – everything's anonymous, secret, everything you do distanced from who you are. Who are you hiding from, Suze? It's not as if you have disapproving parents breathing down your neck." I was on really sensitive territory now. "It's been such a strain for both of us. We've had to tread on eggshells, trying to remember who knows what, and it's kept us apart from our friends. Isn't lack of honesty what you complain about in others?" – I took a deep breath – "your father, for instance."

Her eyes blazed. "Don't you dare..."

But for once I had to dare, and my voice grew stronger. "Suze, you're right in hating the lies he told you and that I've told about you, and I'm not going to do that anymore – I've promised you and I've promised myself. But what about you? Aren't secrets dishonest too? Those frightful weeks when you couldn't speak, haven't they changed anything? Isn't it time for a change? Time you opened up, spoke up, became honest about who you are? Think how strong and free that will make you feel."

We were both still then, me with exhaustion and she with surprise. It was the first time I had challenged the new fiercer Suzie. But I knew I had to confront her difference, or go under.

* * *

That night we slept without touching; each of us keeping as far to our own side of the bed as possible. I wondered if Suzie would ask me to sleep on the sofa, but it seemed things weren't quite as bad as that.

But I was relieved that she was still asleep when I crept out in the morning and let myself out.

My mood wasn't helped by travelling in the dark. I hate this time of year: cold, dank, miserable, spending all my daylight hours at the bank. Still, there was only another week to go. However things were at home, I couldn't wait.

I was glad that the Christmas party was on one of my days off, so I was able to give my excuses without offence. All that kissing under the mistletoe and fawning on the partners who deigned to descend for the occasion. Ugh. Cards arrived in my in-tray from people I saw every day and with whom I had nothing in common. I knew I was being a kill-joy, but I've always moved around too much to get involved with Christmas cards, and in this case, it seemed even sillier. I did have a drink with Andrew and Miles – grateful for their kindness when things had been so tough at home.

I had to remember that even if things with Suzie were difficult now, they were as nothing compared to the Big Silence. In my more rational moments, I knew that there was bound to be a settling down period, but I was exhausted by the roller-coaster that our lives seemed to have become. I tried not to be nostalgic for the days when Bruce was around. I didn't exactly miss him, but life used to be so much quieter! After our latest outburst, things had calmed down again. We still weren't talking much, but Suzie went about with a thoughtful look on her face, and I hoped that she might have taken on board what I'd said, without too much lasting affront. It felt so important that she should find a way forward that excited and didn't threaten her.

I hardly dared broach the subject again, but I needed to have one last go.

"Suze, I've had an idea."

She looked at me with suspicion. "Again."

"Yes, well, I've thought of a way through that might just make it possible. Suppose you just let on who Vox Pop was – that might be enough to get them to trust you – the public really warms to your empathy with people. You are so good at getting people to talk to you – that's a politician's gift. Belinda wouldn't have to come into it at all."

Suzie was silent for a while, then grudgingly acknowledged that I might have a point. "But suppose they recognised me?"

"Why would they, any more than before? The people you've talked to for Vox Pop haven't made the connection, have they?"

"I don't know. I'd have to think about it. Whether Vox Pop would suffer if I went public. I'd need to talk it over with George."

I put my arm round her. I felt her resistance, but she didn't push me away. "Yes, darling, think about it. Don't give up on it. You never know. It might just work."

We had a quiet evening in front of the telly. All this emotional stuff was so draining. But there was a little hope in the air.

* * *

After that I left the subject alone. It was her life, after all. Her business. She buried herself in her Vox Pop work, writing up her notes, drafting the text of the next couple of columns. I too was quiet, going out for solitary cycle rides, pondering her life and mine. The weather was foul and, apart from the bank, there was little for me to do. It was a bit late in the year to get anything moving on the fooling front, but I determined to book some gigs for next year. Time to get organised. So I checked on the closing dates for a couple of the open access festivals, like Nottingham and Buxton. I also needed to see what the others were up to.

A few days later, Suzie surprised me by suggesting a walk. It wasn't usually her kind of thing, especially on a dark drizzly day when hibernation was a more natural response. But I wasn't one to turn down an invitation (saying "yes" is one of the first rules of fooling!), so we donned our waterproofs and ventured out.

"Canal?"

"Okay."

"Brollie?"

"Nah. The wind's a bit strong. We'll manage."

We walked down to the Limehouse Cut and headed towards the point where it meets up with the River Lea. There were few people on the towpath, just a lone man grimly doing his duty by his dog, and a woman doing hers with a pram. The benefits of fresh air. Or maybe just going stir crazy after several days inside. A few swans and coots – or were they moorhens? At Three Mills Island, where the canal opens out, we paused as usual to gaze across the water at the lovely old buildings with their quaint conical roofs. Someone told me that they are some of the oldest recorded tidal mills but I've always been too lazy to check them out. The rain was heavier now, and after a while, I put my hand on Suzie's back.

"Come on."

And, collars up, hands in pockets, we turned round and trudged back, walking into the wind.

"Orbs," said Suzie eventually, "I wanted to say –" She stopped.

"Yes, love?"

"About politicking."

"Yes?"

"Well, when I went through my notes of recent Vox Pop interviews, I realised that I've already got a lot of information I could use. Of course we were discussing particular issues not politics, but people's political opinions naturally come up. It's all part of the same thing. Education, money, benefits – I can see where there might be some possibilities. Looking under the surface, it's amazing how many people have been feeling disenfranchised. Tories with a conscience. Greens and LibDems who don't feel they have a chance. Labour voters who don't like their candidate. And, of course, where there have been shenanigans, pretty well everyone's up in arms. I'd like to think I can do something, but I'm such a novice. I've no idea how to go about things, really."

"At one level, I know it's quite simple. You just have to find ten people in the constituency to support you, and cough up £500. Almost anyone can do it."

We stood aside to let a bedraggled cyclist pass.

"So," I asked, "have you any idea about a possible constituency?"

"Well, there are a few that look possible. Once I've decided – and am really clear I'm going ahead with this – I'll have to get myself an agent. I wish I had some local connections somewhere but I'm sure there are issues – hospitals, recycling – that I know about and can really get behind."

"The crucial thing is that people will be able to see that you're squeaky clean."

"Hmm, hope so. The thing is –" She hesitated at the bottom of the bridge, and turned her rain-spattered face towards me.

"What?"

"I'm nervous, Orbs. No, don't look like that. I am. I'm really happy talking to people in the street – I've been doing it for years – but the idea of getting on a platform and giving a public speech scares the living daylights out of me."

I was astonished. "But all your stage appearances, TV – millions watching you. You have terrific confidence in public."

"Not without Bruce."

Ah yes.

"I have to find my own voice. It's not easy."

I hugged her wet little figure to me. "You will, my Suze, I know you will."

That night Suzie was unusually restless. I woke in the early hours to find her side of the bed empty. I found her in the kitchen, brewing herself some kind of herbal tea.

"Suze?"

"Oh sorry, did I disturb you?"

"No, not at all. Just worried. Are you okay?"

"Can't sleep. Lots on my mind."

The following night was worse. She flailed about, waking me with a cry.

I held her to me. "Darling, you're all right. Suze, you're fine." And then, as she woke and opened her eyes, she gave a great sigh. "Suze? What is it?"

"Oh, a ghastly dream. A nightmare. Standing on a podium with no clothes, talking complete gibberish through a loudspeaker that broadcast my booming voice throughout the universe. You know the sort of thing. What a relief to wake up." I stroked her, we cuddled, and eventually fell asleep in each other's arms.

The next morning, we sat bleary-eyed at the kitchen table with our coffees. I don't think either of us was hungry.

I put my hand on hers. "Poor darling, you had a rotten night, didn't you? Any better this morning?"

She shook her head. "I'm sorry, Orbs, I can't do it."

"Do what, love?"

"Politics."

"Really?"

She shook her head. "It's too soon. I'm just not strong enough to get out there on my own. I have to find my feet. My own two feet. My own voice."

That bloody fox.

"I'm just not ready." Again, she said, "I'm sorry."

"Don't be silly. There's nothing to be sorry about. It's not surprising after all you've been through. And, anyway, it's your business, your life."

But, as I set off for the bank the next day, I did feel let down, I can't deny it. I was used to my strong Suzie, out there, making an impact on the world. And, of course, I've always relied on it too.

Chapter 27

In the midst of all this, my end-of-year review seemed a complete irrelevance. And, given the informal nature of my employment, a mere gesture. But at the appointed time, I took the lift to the seventh floor, and was greeted at the carpeted entrance by Ralph's assistant, who ushered me into the sacred portals.

"Good morning, my boy."

"Good morning, sir – er, Ralph."

"Are you well?"

"Yes, thank you."

"And your parents?"

"Yes, fine, thank you." (Why would he care and how would I know?)

"Good. Sherry?"

And then, as he poured out a thimbleful of *fino* into an elegant ribbed glass, "Thank you."

Formalities over, Ralph placed himself behind his imposing rosewood desk. Referring to the facts and figures on his screen, Ralph ran through the events of the past year as reflected by my attendance.

He then looked at me, and clasped his long-fingered hands on the desk. "Orbs, we've noticed over the past year a pleasing growth not only in your attendance but in commitment to the company."

"Uh, thank you."

"Yes." He cleared his throat. "We've been thinking that maybe it's time to formalise your employment. To offer you a contract at a higher level – a clerk's level – at of course a higher salary."

"Goodness." I wanted to run away. "I don't know what to say. That's very kind, er, generous. I appreciate it." I thought quickly. "Of course, as you know, I do have a lot of outside commitments…"

Ralph smiled benignly. "Yes, of course, Orbs. Perhaps you would like to think about it. With the added responsibility, we would need the assurance of more regular hours, but I'm sure we can come to a mutually beneficial agreement."

"Thank you, yes, I'd like to think about it."

But thinking about it only made it worse. It was just as well that I was on a site visit that afternoon, and had to concentrate on being nice to the client, and paying attention as he fed me the relevant facts and figures. Because, if I stopped for a minute, my mind went all over the place. Ralph's offer was flattering, no doubt, but it felt like a giant iron trap descending from the sky. What was I going to do? What, if anything, was I going to tell Suzie? Here, on a golden platter (a poisoned chalice) was the answer to all our financial worries. Orbs will provide.

* * *

But instead of the iron trap, what actually descended was some manna from heaven. An email from Ranjit. It couldn't have come at a better time. "I'm finally making it to London, just in time for the Solstice. Hope you're up for some fooling. How about asking some of the others? It's been too long."

Yes, it had. Thank God. I was longing to see him and the others. How wonderful to forget my agonies and celebrate the season in our inimitably foolish way. It was high time I reclaimed my community, my tribe – which certainly isn't my colleagues at the bank or my schoolboy chums. It's not even the entertainment world, but this specific group, who share the way I look at the world. When we are together, when we really let go, there's something moving among us, a field, that has a power that's greater than the sum of its parts. I can engage on my own, but when I'm embedded in my group I do it from a much firmer footing.

My foolish mates – how I'd missed them! And what an

opportunity! The least we could do at this so-called festive season was to lighten the load of those miserable Oxford Street shoppers. To lift from them the heaviness of their parcels, their financial anxiety and the weight of others' expectations. And have some fun ourselves. I asked Suzie if she'd like to join us, but she said rather vaguely that she had other things to do.

So, on the day, the Solstice, the shortest day, a cause for celebration in itself, there were just the four of us: Ranjit and myself and Lucy and Chuck who had come down by train from Brum, where they'd been working at a children's hospital, and were looking forward to a bit of light relief. We gathered at my flat for a much-needed catch-up, consumed hastily assembled cheese and pickle sandwiches to sustain the inner fool and then got into costume – with our own rather bizarre variations on Christmas elves. Chuck, a very small young man, had a very large pointed hat with a bell on it, Ranjit, a silk waistcoat several sizes too small for his broad frame, with big bulbous pantaloons in shiny gold, Lucy in a little flowery frock, bright red lips to match her nose, and outsize shoes. My own costume was slightly more traditional, using my multi-purpose stripy leggings and a half-and-half green-and-red button-through jacket. We dressed in silence and with serious intent and, before going through the door, put on our noses. We stood for a while facing each other in stillness, then grinned and ventured out on the streets.

As always, it took a little time to let go of the need to do anything, to know that our presence alone makes an impact, that less is more. We stood at a crossing, waving at passing cars, then crossing the road in any way we felt moved – in single file or linking arms: big steps, backwards, hopping, or in an exaggeratedly normal fashion, then turned round and waved at cars before the lights changed and we crossed again. By the time we got to Oxford Circus, we were in fine fettle, making straight for a couple of guys with drum and guitar and a begging bowl. We danced, inviting any willing passers-by to join us.

The crowds of miserable trudgers began to be dotted about with newly light-hearted prancers. Small children forgot their weariness and danced with delight, while middle-aged women up for the day from Dorset or Slough put down their shopping to take selfies to show their friends.

It's hard to say what we did. It was all so incredibly silly, as we responded singly or together to any slight incident or invitation that took our fancy. Seeing an exit sign leaning against a lamppost and pointing upwards, we scrambled and slithered on the lamppost, trying to obey the instruction. We laughed a lot, and tried to share it around.

When we got back to the flat, Suzie was still out. With suitable gravity, we took off our noses, and divested ourselves of our costumes, then over a cup of tea had a good laugh about the afternoon's activities. Chuck and Lucy had a train to catch, so they didn't hang around but it was good to have a little time alone with Ranjit, a chance to hear what he had been up to. As he downed a cuppa, he was in buoyant mood.

"Actually, Orbs, I'm pretty excited. I've just done a funding application for something we might do as a group, and I actually think we might get the money."

I put down my mug. "Really? What's it for?"

"Well, it's an arts festival. Can I tell you about it?"

It did sound exciting. "Oh, please do, Ranjit."

"Well, I'm not spreading the word till we know we've got the money, but I'm hoping it's something a few of us might do. I'm calling our group 'Some Fools' – quite good, don't you think? And calling our act 'Invitation'. Anyway, the idea is to be alongside any other activity in the festival. Here –" He dug around inside his satchel and pulled out the application. "I brought it with me."

Under "You and your work" I read:

We offer to be alongside any other activity – dance, pottery – to add texture and context to whatever is going on. It is based on spontaneity and seeing the world afresh.

"Terrific. Love it."

Then I read on.

Whereas anxiety tends to focus around fears of being out of control and apprehension about what might or might not happen in the future, the Fool inhabits the present moment, seeing life through eyes of wonder and openness. In a sense the Fool is already "out of control", but embraces this rather than fearing it, thus demonstrating a healthy and playful alternative to anxious living.

I was bemused. "What's all this about anxiety? Not sure I get that."

"Oh, sorry, it's an arts festival, but linked to a mental health charity."

"Oh." That was a facer.

"Read to the end, then you'll get it."

This can be immensely freeing and relaxing, and this is the position from which we would seek to engage with people, inviting them to rediscover their own sense of authenticity and playfulness.

Yes, that spoke to me. That is what we do.

"Wow, Ranjit, that's amazing. For a silent fool, you're pretty good with words!"

Ranjit smiled with pleasure. "What do you think?"

I tried to hide my discomfort. "Well, it sounds wonderful. But pretty high powered. Are we really up to it?"

"Well, you have to ramp it up to get the funding."

"I suppose. But do you think we will? There must be lots of competition."

"Yes, but nothing like this. The fact that we don't rely on language is a big plus – it's an international festival, and we can 'speak' to anyone."

Yes. I could see that. It might just work. Even if the idea terrified me.

I thought it was time to tell Ranjit what had been going on in my life. It was such a relief to let it out at last. He didn't try to give advice but listened to me in silence and with a grave attention. So now, finally, there was someone who had an inkling of what I'd been going through. Even if I didn't spell it out, he would perhaps understand how uncertain I felt about any plans for the future.

I walked him to the tube, and we gave each other a hug. With his big frame and big coat, it was indeed like a bear hug.

"So," he said, with concern, "will you be all right?"

"Yes, I think so. Things at home seem to be settling down. It's helped so much to be able to talk to you, and what you're planning sounds amazing, really creative. Just let me get my head around it. I'd so love to work with you again."

When I got back to the flat, I was knackered. What an afternoon! Suze had returned and was, I was relieved to see, in a mellow mood. I hadn't the energy to deal with anything difficult.

I gave her a quick kiss. "We've just had tea. Like some?"

"Oh, yes, please. Builder's."

"Mince pie?"

"Oh, I don't –"

"Oh, come on, Suzie, you need to build up your strength."

"Hardly."

She's always watching her weight – goodness knows why – but it's an obsession with the women in this business. But after all those weeks when she couldn't be bothered to eat, she is thinner than she ought to be. Anyway, on this occasion, it didn't take much arm-twisting. She likes mince pies.

I put a mug and plate on the table for her, sat down, and helped myself to some more.

Suzie remained standing, her hand on the back of my chair. "So, was it a good afternoon?"

I stretched my legs out under the table. "Tiring but, yes, brilliant. We had such fun. And it was really good to have a chance to chat to Ranjit. It's been too long."

"Yes, I know. I'm so pleased he could come." She looked down on me with a welcome fondness, and twirled a lock of my hair in her fingers. "I'm so glad you're staying with your fooling. I worried that I might have put you off silence."

"Well," I said with a grin, "there's silence and silence."

"Oh, you!" She reached for a cushion and aimed at my head.

I ducked. "No, seriously. I wouldn't know what to do with words. Fooling is my practice. I'm just thinking of how I might do it in a different way."

"Oh?"

"Yes. I'm not political like you, Suzie, but I do want to make a difference in some way. A foolish way, if possible."

"What are you thinking of?"

It was too early to talk about it. I needed to mull it over first. "Not sure I am yet, but Ranjit and I talked about something we might do together. A bit challenging, but I'm sure we'll sort something out."

Suzie nodded reassuringly. "I'm sure you will." She paused. "Orbs, that reminds me."

"What?"

"The bank statement came in."

"Oh, God." Down with a bang. How on earth could that remind her?

"Don't worry. It's not too bad. There's still quite a bit from B&BQs, but we need to be careful. There's so much going on. It'll take a while for both of us to find our feet, and we're going to need some money."

And how.

"I've been thinking. We've got that old problem of time and money. You're never going to be able to explore anything while you're still toiling away at the bank. So, I was thinking that it wouldn't hurt me to dust off my old skills and do a bit of reporting. That way you can cut down the number of days you do at the bank. Fair shares."

"Really?"

She smiled and nodded. I stood up and took her in my arms.

"What a generous offer, Suze. What a love you are."

It was, and she is. But after the initial teary gratitude, my euphoria subsided. The afternoon's play had been wonderfully refreshing, but that funding application had hit a nerve. It would take time to absorb it. I still hadn't told Suzie about Ralph's offer at the bank, and her generosity now only increased my discomfort. After she'd gone to bed, I sat up late, looking out at the night sky and asking for answers.

It was lovely of Suzie to care about my future, but, actually, being given this much freedom terrified me. I knew I wanted to do something. I just wished I knew what it was. Justice. Yes, but what and how? I'm not political, and in any case, I've no intention of treading on Suzie's heels. The only party that would suit me (probably the only one that would have me) is the Monster Raving Loony Party. Actually, I had a look at their manifesto the other day. Their mixture of political satire and pure silliness is absolutely spot on – **"We will stand on a platform of free woolly hats for all, so that we can pull the wool over people's eyes"** – but there's no money there, and what part could I play without speaking? I suppose I could at least join them and show my solidarity, but in practical terms there had to be something else.

So, then I forced myself to acknowledge that what was really terrifying me was this plan of Ranjit's. "Out of control." Was that what we were? It had always been precisely his lack of control, his unpredictability, that had frightened me about Freddie, that had made me run for cover. That Ranjit was finding similarities between us was doing my head in.

I wanted more than anything to work with Ranjit and the others. I was fed up with struggling to do everything on my own, but if I got involved, it would force me to confront something I'd been avoiding all my life. Could I face it? If I funked it, I'd feel even more of a useless appendage than I did already. Of course we might not get the funding. And, even if it did come off and I did go for it, it would hardly solve our money problems. But that wasn't really the point.

* * *

My annual review seemed light years away, and completely irrelevant. But I would have to give them an answer and, after a brief struggle with my lesser self, I knew I had to tell Suzie too. I owed it to her. She was so caught up in Vox Pop that it was hard to find the right time but, after supper one night, as she settled in front of her computer, I managed to broach the subject.

I leant against the wall and tried to adopt a nonchalant air. "I had my annual review the other day."

Suzie didn't look up. "Uh-huh? The usual? Five minutes in and out?"

"No, actually. They had something to say."

Then she did raise her head. "Oh? What?"

"They've offered me a more established job, higher level, more pay."

Her eyes widened. "Oh, Orbs, that's great."

"You think?"

"Of course. That means they really rate you."

Pause.

"Of course you can't possibly accept it."

Thank God. "No?"

"No. Of course not." She swivelled on her chair to face me, her eyes bright with emotion. "You'd be crushed. Where would all your dreams be then?"

I said feebly, "But this could solve all our money problems...," I tailed off, knowing that my voice lacked conviction.

"Don't even think of it. We'll find some other way."

"You think?"

"I know."

And I know why I love her. My generous woman. After all she's been through.

Chapter 28

I'm off now till the New Year. It's a huge relief, of course it is, but it's very odd having all this time. We're active people. Our jobs usually take us all over the place, so we rarely get to spend more than a few days at a time at home. We're not used to all this sitting around, or spending all this time in each other's company. We just don't know what to do with ourselves. I could send off for some boxed sets, but even though this is hibernatory weather, after the past few months we're sick and tired of being inside, and don't just want to sit around all the time. We've had the odd meal out, which was very enjoyable but in general we don't go to anything special. I know that's a bit pathetic in a city like London where there's so much going on, but we're used to providing the entertainment, not watching it.

This evening, as usual, there was nothing on the box, so Suzie suggested a game. "Cards, Scrabble?"

"Suzie, we're not 90. What do you want for Christmas? A jigsaw?" She threw a mock punch.

Christmas. Oh God. We're too late.

Before I met Suzie, I avoided Christmas as much as I could, and made a point of being at the opposite end of the country from my parents. The mixture of ramrod backs and emotional blackmail would, I know, have defeated me. Not to mention Freddie's unpredictable behaviour – always worse under festive pressure.

This is our second Christmas together, and last year we were still so starry-eyed that it was lovely to spend it alone with each other. We wouldn't have wanted it any other way. So there was no pressure to get involved with family. In the past, we'd each of us been busy in our various social and work circles; this year we feel rather isolated. If we'd got our act together, we could have volunteered at Crisis or something. But, with all that had gone on over the autumn, Christmas was hardly at the top of our list. Now it was too late.

Of course, I couldn't be unaware that Christmas was on its way. Everyone had been going on about it at work, some cards had found their way through our own front door, and it had been coming at us from every direction since November. In fact, the publicity had been so relentless and had gone on for so long that after a while I'd simply failed to see it. My eyes and ears glazed over and by the time I paid attention, the moment had almost passed.

I can't say I was sorry. In fact, I was probably deliberately blocking it. From every shop window and every TV ad came the message that this is a family time, and that wasn't a message I wanted to hear. And I knew exactly what Suzie was doing when she spread the fingers of her right hand in front of her, contemplated her nails and nonchalantly asked: "So, what are we going to do for Christmas?"

"I hate to tell you, Suze, but we're too late to do anything. Tomorrow's Christmas Eve."

Suzie looked at me with dismay. "Really? Is it?" Her sense of time was still unreliable.

"It doesn't matter. The twenty-fifth is a pretty random date anyway."

"But I wanted to buy stuff, prepare things."

"Don't worry, darling, you don't need to get things. Let's just do it late, and make it as Christmassy as possible. After all, there's a lot to celebrate."

She smiled uncertainly "That seems a bit odd, but I suppose we could. What about doing it at New Year instead?"

"Yes, great." I warmed to the idea. It's a very foolish notion doing things on an unconventional day. Fireworks in August, carols in May. What's Christmas to a fool? Like any other day, it's an opportunity to play. The only day we hang on to is our day: April 1. If we don't manage to get together at other times we try to make April Fool's Day a special one. The gang was already planning for next year. Some sort of mayhem in Edinburgh.

But in the meantime, here we were.

"So what shall we do?"

I shrugged. "Dunno. Nothing much. Just have some time together."

"You don't want to go anywhere?"

"No, I'd rather not. Everywhere's so crowded. And expensive."

"Yes." She considered. "I could cook."

"That would be nice."

"Do you want to invite anybody?" She wasn't fooling anyone.

"No. Our friends will be organised elsewhere by now. And I'd rather just be with you." As she took a breath, I said, "And before you ask, Suzie, I'm not inviting Freddie." Still less my parents.

She took it philosophically. Doubtless no more than she'd expected.

The following day I rang my mother, to avoid her waking us with an early morning call.

"Happy Christmas, Mum."

"And to you, darling. But it's tomorrow."

"Yes, we're going to be busy tomorrow, so I thought I'd catch you now."

"Ah, so we won't be seeing you?"

"I'm sorry. You know how things are."

"Well, you know how much I'd like to have a family Christmas. All of us together."

I tried to make the right noises. I hoped, as ever, to speak to my father, but Mother avoided it, saying that he simply wouldn't hear what I had to say. But I would have heard him.

It was good to have some extra days to prepare for our celebration. When I woke on the morning of the official day, I couldn't help remembering all the festive Christmases that were going on all over the country, and feeling rather smug that in our household the day would pass almost without notice.

But I had reckoned without Suzie. As I stretched beside her sleeping form, I felt something heavy at the foot of the bed. I sat up, and discovered a Christmas stocking. Well, when I say stocking, it was a voluminous felt boot, big enough for a Christmas giant, plastered with multi-coloured felt shapes of reindeer, Father Christmas and snowflakes. And, inside, walnuts wrapped in foil, tangerines, a multitude of little wrapped shapes. Heavens, how had she found the time?

Suzie stirred and smiled sleepily. "I hope you don't mind, Orbs. I know you don't want presents, and that you want to wait until New Year, and we will, but I couldn't bear the day to pass without giving you something."

I was touched. "Oh, sweetie, thank you. You are a darling." I would have prolonged the kiss, but Suzie gently pushed me away. She wanted to explain.

"You see, that's my best memory of childhood – those mornings when a stocking magically arrived on my bed. Christmas wouldn't be Christmas without magic."

"And I have nothing for you."

"Oh, we agreed no presents and I know that anything special has to wait until 'our' day."

And this time the kiss was given time to develop.

* * *

Christmas or not, I was looking forward to creating a celebratory event for us both, and was determined to make it as much of a treat as possible – not least to celebrate Suzie's recovery. What a year we had had.

When everyone else had moved on to talk of sales, slimming and holidays, it was a bit hard to keep up any sense of anticipation. We found ourselves avoiding television, suspending ourselves in our own little bubble of time. At least I did. Suzie was out and about a good deal – which was hardly surprising after being cooped up for all that time. Some days she went up West to shop (rather her than me) but surprisingly she spent much of the time round at Hannah's place. This new enthusiasm seemed a bit strange but she probably liked having a friend living near by and Hannah's faithful companionship during the Big Silence must have drawn them together. And though Suzie seemed oblivious to their lovely little cat, she seemed to enjoy the children.

Anyway, I was pleased that I again had some time to myself in the flat. Time off work, time when I didn't have to consider anyone else, and could eat what I liked. Time to breathe, to contemplate, and consider what I might do next. I dug out all my fooling clothes and props from the trunk, threw away a pair of pantaloons that were past their sell-by date, and made a list of props that I might add to my collection. I tried to put Ranjit's proposal out of my mind. It might never happen.

I also needed the time to prepare some "Christmas" surprises for Suzie. Over the past few months it had been hard to find anywhere to be private in our little flat. As we had rarely both been around at the same time, it hadn't been an issue till now.

And I caught up a little with the chores, including the washing up. Reluctant though I am to admit it, I know that sometimes doing something practical can keep me in the present tense, so while Suzie was out one afternoon, I decided to tackle the stack of dirty plates and pans. We've no room for a dishwasher, and, anyway, we're away too much for it to be worth having one. In general, our agreement is that whoever cooks doesn't wash up, but during the period of Suzie's incapacitation, I'd got used to doing it – eventually – trying to turn it into an opportunity for mindfulness.

When Suzie came in, she was full of her visit to Hannah. She flung her coat on the settee, came up behind me and put her arms round my waist. My hands in the suds, I leaned back gratefully into the softness of her embrace.

"Nice visit?"

"Yes, lovely. Subeer is such a little love, isn't he?"

"Shy, though."

"Yes, I guess. But he's come out of his shell a bit. We built a little brick house today. For such a little one he's really good with his hands."

"And Hannah?"

"Oh, she was fine. Busy, as ever."

I tipped out the water and dried my hands. "I sometimes wonder what you two have to talk about."

Suzie looked surprised. "Oh, any number of things. She's an interesting woman. She's got an MBA, you know."

"No, I didn't." Everyone, it seems, is more qualified than me.

"Yes. She's just waiting till Subeer goes to school and Lali's a bit older, then she's planning to go back to work."

"Palash?"

"Yes, fine, I think. He works long hours, apparently, and doesn't see much of the kids.

I sense Hannah's a bit frustrated, though she would never say so."

And I sensed that Hannah's support during the Big Silence had formed a strong bond between the two women, though, again, neither of them would ever say so.

Chapter 29

On New Year's Eve, in best "Christmas" tradition, Suzie got up early (well, for us that's about 10:30 a.m.) to prepare the meal. When I rolled over to find her space empty, I was a bit disgruntled. So much for my morning inclinations: the best way to start such a special day. But then Suzie came in carrying two cups of coffee.

"Merry sort of Christmas," I said.

She smiled, "And the same to you. Careful!", she said as I reached out for her, and she set the mugs down on the bedside table before getting back into bed. "I can't be long, there's a meal to prepare."

There was all the time in the world for that.

By mutual consent, we dressed up, I in my wine-coloured velvet waistcoat and slinky trousers in an absurd lime green; Suzie breath-taking in a low-cut sparkly floor-length black dress. I was hungry just looking at her.

The meal was to be vegetarian, of course, as there was no point in cooking two meals. I was in charge of laying the table. So, I used a white sheet as a tablecloth, and put out our best (well, our only) cutlery, crockery and glasses. I opened the wine. Maybe, for once, Suzie would have some. It looked pretty festive, with my home-made crêpe paper crackers and a centrepiece of a candle surrounded by a bunch of glorious red leaves that I found in the park. I blew up some balloons and pinned them round the walls of the room.

Suzie brought in the nut roast and started to cut it up as I fetched the rest of the dishes from the kitchen.

I poured us each some wine and we sat down and smiled into each other's eyes.

I raised my glass. "Cheers."

"Cheers."

We raised and clinked our glasses. It all felt a bit formal, odd, stilted. Not our usual form. But we relaxed when we began to eat. I was really hungry, and the meal was pretty good. A loaf made of all sorts of mushrooms – "Hope you didn't pick these yourself!" – cranberries and nuts. And all the trimmings. Roast potatoes, sprouts, Christmas pud and brandy butter. For all our scepticism, where food is concerned, you can't beat traditional.

The fun really started when we pulled the crackers. Pulling them was rather hard work – there was a lot of puffing and blowing – but they did make a noise in the end. And burst open with a jolt so that the contents scattered all over the table. I had taken a lot of trouble to find the little bits and pieces, and made sure that Suzie got the lion's share. Some silly naval-style paper hats that we both put on – hers in a becoming lilac, mine in a shocking pink. A whistle, a little mirror, a couple of truffles and, pride of place, some tiny plastic loudhailers (well, maybe they were funnels, but they served the purpose) through which we could shout at each other across the table.

I picked one up, and shouted, "Ahoy there, HMS Silliness calling!"

Suzie picked up the other little loudhailer. "Ahoy there, HMS Silliness!"

"I have a message for Suzie Tavener."

Suzie could hardly speak for laughing. "Go ahead, HMS Silliness."

"Aubrey De'Ath Grimsby-Grenville sends his love."

"And Suzie Tavener wants him to know that she sends hers."

"Over and out."

We ended up, of course, in bed. We were nicely oiled, and we needed a rest after all that eating.

We rolled out of bed about five. It was dark by then, so we could have stayed put, but Suzie was insistent that it was time for tea.

I reluctantly propped myself up on one elbow. "I'll bring you a cup."

"No, we need to get up and have a proper tea."

I groaned. "Come on, Suze, I'm still stuffed from lunch."

But I obediently staggered to my feet, drew on a dressing gown, had a pee and sat myself down at the table. Suzie was bustling around in the kitchen. She had put out two little plates and now brought out, to my amazement, a sumptuous and obviously home-made Christmas cake.

"Suzie? Did you make this?"

She nodded with a modest pleasure.

I looked at it with astonishment. It was big and square and iced as well, with a little red post box on the top. "I didn't know you knew how to. How did you manage to do it without my knowing?"

"Well, it was Hannah who taught me. And I made it round there."

Ah, so that was why she spent all that time there.

"You sneaky thing! But, Hannah? She's a Muslim."

"What's that got to do with it? They celebrate Christmas as a secular festival like the rest of us. The more festivals the merrier."

"Well I never. And she knows how to make Christmas cake? How bizarre."

"Not really. Come on – that woman who won *Bake Off*, she was a Muslim, wasn't she? Anyway, apparently Hannah's mother always used to make one in Bangladesh, and she's made one too, to take to her sister. Though she started a lot earlier, so that she could feed it properly."

Whatever that meant. "Well, thank you and her. I'm touched, honoured."

As she cut a couple of slices from the cake, Suzie removed the little red post box and put it on my plate. "And that's for you."

As I looked more closely, I saw that there was a tiny roll of paper protruding from the box. Suzie was ostentatiously looking away and, remembering another message all those weeks ago, I knew that this too was significant. My heart thudding, I unrolled the paper. And this one, also in Suzie's handwriting, said: "The word 'silly' comes from the German *selig*, meaning blessed."

And the cake was scrumptious too.

* * *

We turned on the telly in time for the New Year countdown and the bongs, and watched the excited crowds on the Embankment. Much as I like fireworks, I was mightily relieved not to be among the penned-in masses. Home was fine. Just fine. The two of us sat in a mellow mood well into the early hours, our limbs entwined, swilling our wine and letting various bits of nonsense pass before our eyes. Contentment.

Suzie put her glass down with a yawn. "Oof, I'm stiff." She disentangled herself and stretched her arms and legs.

"Time for bed, I think." And for once I meant sleep. I was knackered.

"Mmm. Do you mind if I use the bathroom first?"

"No, go ahead."

When I clambered into bed, Suzie was already snuggling down.

"Ow, your feet are cold."

"Yes, but yours are lovely and warm!"

Just as I was turning my mind towards sleep, Suzie suddenly remembered something.

"Oh, Orbs, I meant to say." She sounded unnaturally perky.

"Mmm?"

"You know I mentioned going back to reporting?"

Oh, not now. For goodness' sake, Suze, don't you ever want to sleep? I rolled over and reluctantly recovered my consciousness. "Yes. Why? Have you changed your mind?" And then, even more reluctantly, "I wouldn't blame you."

"No, I've got a better plan. I went to see Geoff the other day."

"Geoff?" I was properly awake now. "Oh, the political editor. I thought you were avoiding him."

"Yes, I was. But, given all the sexual hoo-hah that's gone on, he wouldn't dare chance his arm. And, anyway, I've made it pretty clear that if he tried anything I wouldn't hesitate to blow a whistle or anything else that came to hand."

I laughed and nuzzled her shoulder. "Good for you."

Suzie eased herself up on to one elbow. She had obviously had too much coffee and was properly into her stride. "Anyway, I've been thinking about the politics idea and I like it. But not yet. I really haven't got the guts to put myself out there in such a big way. And if I leave it for a while, there's less chance of anyone recognising me from B&BQs, and there'll be time for memories to fade. I'm not sure I'm up to it, but I'm beginning to realise it would be good to do something that I don't have to keep quiet about." She gulped, and I held her to me.

Goodness, that's progress. But Suzie as a politician. It isn't just her that needs time to assimilate that. It will take some getting used to. "Suze, you are one brave woman. You've no idea how I admire you."

She smiled a little wanly. "Thanks, Orbs. Well, I think Geoff feels sad about B&B – it was his idea, after all. Anyway, he suggested something else."

Drily. "Quite an ideas man, our Geoff."

"You know *From our Home Correspondent*, that UK spinoff of *From our Own Correspondent*?"

"Never heard it, but heard *of* it, yes."

"It's not his programme, but with my track record he thinks he could get me on to the team. He'll have a word with the producer."

"Wow! That's a great idea. Have you done any radio?"

"Yes, in my reporting days, quite a bit, actually. I rather like it. And, of course, these programmes will build on the work I'm already doing for Vox Pop. Fits perfectly."

"And, for once, it'll be work that you can claim as yours. It'll have the Suzie Tavener name attached."

"Yes. Not that it matters. But, anyway, that's me sorted. Now it's time to concentrate on you."

I rolled away and averted my face. "What about me?"

"We never talk about your plans. Where you are with things."

"I'm all over the place." The truth.

"You never did tell me what you talked about with Ranjit."

I shut my eyes. "No."

Suzie put her hand on my cheek. "Orbs?"

Oh God. This was so hard. "It's difficult, Suze. I haven't really come to terms with it."

"With what?"

"Whether I'm up to it."

"Join the club."

I rolled back to face her. "Yes, I suppose so." Pause. "You see, Ranjit has done an application for a festival."

"Sounds good."

"With a mental health charity."

"Ah."

"Yes. I'm scared. Scared of what I might discover."

My heart was thudding. Neither of us spoke.

Then, Suzie put her hand on the back of my neck and looked into my eyes in the gloom. "You know why I fell in love with you?"

I looked back then, finding it hard to catch my breath. "Apart from my boyish good looks, you mean?"

A token smile. "Yes, apart from them."

"No, I've never known. Never understood. You are –"

"No, Orbs, we're talking about you. Apart from your support of me, which has been wonderful, you have a stillness, a deep sense of yourself. In our best moments I feel at peace, safe with you."

After a while I said, "Thank you." And wished I could believe it.

"And if it hadn't been for you, I might well have got sucked into all that celebrity nonsense. You see through it."

I raised my eyebrows, but said nothing in reply.

"So, what can we do, how can we change things, so that you can feel like that more of the time?"

We've never talked like this, well, not since the beginning. "Well, I think" (and God knows I had been thinking) "that I'm never going to make my living as a fool."

"I'm sure you could if you really put more into it. Really made an effort to get yourself known."

"Yes, but that's just it. I'm not that kind of person. I'm no good at the organising, pushing myself on social media and all that stuff. I just don't like it."

"But fooling is what you love, that's when you are most you." She smiled. "And we need one of us to keep up the fun."

"Yes, but in a way doing it for money destroys the whole point of it. Maybe I have to accept that that's for love, and find something else for money. Keep the fooling for" – smile – "for best."

"And the bank?"

"Well, it's odd, but I've been happier there recently – got to know people a bit – but it's never going to be my thing. You know that."

Suzie's eyes were grave. "Yes, I do."

"This plan of Ranjit's, it may not come off and it would only be a festival anyway. Not a way of life." I was trying to persuade myself. I knew only too well that if I did it, there was a danger that it would turn my world upside down. "I'll have to see what happens."

The lovemaking that followed was just that, making, re-creating, our love, in every movement. Gentle, ecstatic, and overwhelming.

Just as I was finally slipping into sleep, Suzie murmured

something.

"Orbs?"

"Mmm. Yes?"

"What do you think...how would you feel...about trying for a baby?"

OMG.

I had no idea where this had come from but knew that it would change my universe. "I...I'd be delighted," was what I finally said before we held each other and kissed, and at last we slept.

* * *

I'd hoped for some time to think, but Suzie returned to the subject over a late breakfast. "Your parents would be pleased, wouldn't they?" she asked slyly. "All parents long for grandchildren."

Ho-hum. Thoughts of Suzie's father crossed my mind, and I wondered.

"We could ask Freddie to be godfather."

Over my dead body.

But, as I was shaving, the reality overtook me. The commitment that Suzie was making, the fact that she believed in us as a lasting unit. That I was good enough. I was overwhelmed. With soap still lingering on my chin, I came out into the sitting room and tried to take her in my arms. "Oh, my darling, thank you."

But Suzie held me off. "There's just one thing, Orbs. No jealousy."

"Jealousy? Of course not." But I knew what she meant. "No, Suze, this is different. This would be for both of us. My baby as well as yours. You know."

Suzie looked away. "Yes. I know. I'm sorry. I've realised all sorts of things, and it – these past weeks – it hasn't been easy. I realise that with Bruce," she swallowed, "with puppets, I've been hiding."

Then she looked back at me with her enchanting smile. "We'll be different, won't we? We've changed."

I smiled back. "Yes." It would not be easy but I knew we would both try. She to share and I to trust. Time I grew up. I'd begun to take responsibility, and now I could see that this was just the beginning.

I know you should never have a baby to save a relationship but I was beginning to think that it might be the answer. That we need a third person for our relationship to work. It's what we're used to, after all.

We'll just have to wait and see.

Chapter 30

I put on my costume, mindfully, taking care with each item. Noticing the feeling of material against skin as I slipped off my jeans and T-shirt and donned purple pantaloons and a stripy green-and-white top. As I eased on to my toes, then heels, my green socks with big pink hearts. And last of all perched my pork pie hat on top of my straggly hair. Pressed it down, so that it would stay put. Decided against the nose.

I paused at the front door and took a breath, collecting, gathering myself. Pause and remember who you are. I opened the door and crossed the threshold.

A woman across the road was unpacking her car.

She looked up and viewed me with concern. "Are you all right?"

I nodded.

"Do you know where you're going?"

I nodded again, but I don't think she believed me.

I made my way to the little corner shop and picked up a bunch of daffodils, and stood there, looking around. A shop assistant came up to me and asked, again with careful concern, "Would you like me to show you how to use the self-checkout?" I let her, let her feel good about helping someone she obviously thought was decidedly less than. Bizarre, these responses because actually my costume is not so way out – all bought at ordinary clothing stalls.

On the way home, I gave one flower to a startled passer-by, then went over to a stationery taxi, and knocked on the window. The driver wound it down with misgiving showing on his face. I proffered a flower, which he took, and then delved into his pocket. "Collecting for charity, are you? How much?"

I shook my head.

"Don't want any money?"

I shook my head.

"You mean you're just going round giving flowers away?"

I beamed and nodded.

"Weird. Well, thank you."

He shook his head in disbelief and drove away.

At home I carefully took off and hung up my costume and sat for a while.

* * *

So here we are, dreaming of a future in which Suzie is speaking with her own voice at last, Freddie and Bruce are making what they will of theirs and I thankfully and purposefully without mine. For me, to coin a phrase, the sound of silence.

EPILOGUE

I

A white van drove up the long gravel driveway, and stopped outside the farmhouse door. A handsome young man with a shock of black hair jumped down from the passenger seat and opened the back doors of the van.

The driver followed him round the back of the farmhouse and they made several journeys back and forth, carrying boxes. When they had packed the last of them into the back of the van, the driver closed the doors and the young man went once more to the back door of the house.

"Now, dear," called a prim elderly voice from inside, "be careful. Please ring me when you get there."

"Yes, Mother, I will. I'll be fine."

"Make sure you take your pills."

"Yes, Mother" (*not*).

"And keep in touch."

"Yes, of course."

The young man reappeared and climbed into the passenger seat, waving out of the window as the van drew away. As they approached the gates at the bottom of the drive, he reached into his satchel and drew out a sleek long puppet. He stroked the fox's fur. "Just you and me now, mate," said Freddie. "Oh, and Gulliver too."

II

"Would you like a story, Jamie?"

"Yes, yes, Mummy, I would."

"What shall we read?"

"The three bears," shouted the little boy, jumping up and down on the bed.

"Goldilocks? Really? Wouldn't you rather have something

different for once?"

"No, no, Mummy, the three bears."

"All right," said Suzie," but only if you will get into bed."

"Orrright." And Jamie got in between the sheets and waited with barely suppressed impatience, while Suzie collected three bears from the cupboard and put them on the bed. The old big floppy one from her own childhood; the little stiff hard one from the pound shop, and the smooth-haired medium-sized one who sat up nicely and seemed to pay attention.

"So," said Suzie, sitting down on the bed, "Once upon a time there were three little bears: Daddy Bear, Mummy Bear, and Baby Bear." As she named them, Jamie picked up each bear in turn and made them give a little bow.

"Who's been eating my porridge?" asked Daddy Bear in a deep voice.

"Who's been eating my porridge?" asked Mummy Bear in a Mummy-ish sort of voice.

"Who's been eating my porridge?" squeaked Baby Bear.

Jamie moved the bears around as they spoke. He knew it was them speaking because it wasn't Mummy. Her lips didn't move except when she was telling the story.

"...and away she ran, down the stairs and out into the forest. And she never went there again."

Suzie closed the book and began to gather up the bears. Jamie held on to Daddy Bear and clutched him to his chest. With a smile, Suzie put the other bears in the cupboard, tucked the duvet round the still excited little boy, and gave him a kiss. "Come on, Jamie. Sleep time now. Uncle Freddie's coming tomorrow."

"But I want more. I want to know what happened."

Acknowledgements

I would like to thank the following people for sharing their expertise: Geoffrey Durham, Jake Eiseman-Renyard, Angela Halvorson-Bogo, Chris McClelland, Rod Reeken, Vicky Tedder, Claire Thompson, and Sarah White. All errors are my own.

The Author

Jennifer Kavanagh worked in publishing for nearly thirty years, the last fourteen as an independent literary agent. In the past fifteen years she has run a community centre in London's East End, worked with homeless street people and refugees, and set up microcredit programmes in London and in Africa. She has also worked as a research associate for the Prison Reform Trust and currently facilitates workshops for conflict resolution both in prison and in the community. Jennifer contributes regularly to the Quaker Press, and is an associate tutor at Woodbrooke Quaker study centre. She is a Churchill Fellow, a Fellow of the Royal Society of Arts and a member of a community of fools. She lives in London.

"Jennifer is one of the most interesting writers of our generation on spirituality."
—Derek A. Collins, London Centre for Spirituality

The Emancipation of B

B is not a child of his time. As an outsider, he hides his secrets well. Freedom is all he dreams of. But when it comes at last, it is in the most unexpected way – and at a considerable cost.

Jennifer Kavanagh's first novel.

A small interior novel about redemption that reveals itself slowly but irresistibly.

"In an age that overwhelmingly favours extraversion, Jennifer Kavanagh has done a quietly defiant thing, to craft a genuine adventure of the inward life. To outward eyes a 'sad loner', its hero resists all clichés and his journey holds us, not least because his consciousness is rendered in prose as crisp and calm and spare as poetry."
—Philip Gross, winner of the T.S. Eliot Poetry Prize 2009

"A hymn to mindfulness and a moving meditation on our conflicting ideas of home in a novel that explores one solitary man's efforts to find sanctuary in the most unlikely of places."
—Paul Wilson, author of *The Visiting Angel*

"This is a beautifully written novel with a haunting central character. As I became more absorbed by B, I became fearful for him; at the end, wanting to know what might happen next. On reflection, the story challenges us to reconsider more honestly our relationships with people and with the world around us, to turn away from the frenzy of contemporary living towards a simplicity of being."
—*Magnet* magazine

"Compelling and wise – It has been a long time since a novel captured my imagination in the way that this one has... What a gem – A wonderful book which stays in the mind long after reading – It is at times gripping, empathetic, sensitive, full of real insights and a fantastic read – Enthralling – A superb record of a journey to wholeness and connection – This is one of the most original books I've ever read."

— Excerpts from other reviews

978-1-78279-884-2 (Paperback) £7.99 $13.95

978-1-78279-883-5 (ebook) £2.99 $4.9

FICTION

Put simply, we publish great stories. Whether it's literary or popular, a gentle tale or a pulsating thriller, the connecting theme in all Roundfire fiction titles is that once you pick them up you won't want to put them down.
If you have enjoyed this book, why not tell other readers by posting a review on your preferred book site.

Recent bestsellers from Roundfire are:

The Bookseller's Sonnets
Andi Rosenthal
The Bookseller's Sonnets intertwines three love stories with a tale of
religious identity and mystery spanning five hundred years and
three countries.
Paperback: 978-1-84694-342-3 ebook: 978-184694-626-4

Birds of the Nile
An Egyptian Adventure
N.E. David
Ex-diplomat Michael Blake wanted a quiet birding trip up the Nile
– he wasn't expecting a revolution.
Paperback: 978-1-78279-158-4 ebook: 978-1-78279-157-7

Blood Profit$
The Lithium Conspiracy
J. Victor Tomaszek, James N. Patrick, Sr.
The blood of the many for the profits of the few… *Blood Profit$* will
take you into the cigar-smoke-filled room where American policy
and laws are really made.
Paperback: 978-1-78279-483-7 ebook: 978-1-78279-277-2

The Burden
A Family Saga
N.E. David
Frank will do anything to keep his mother and father apart. But
he's carrying baggage – and it might just weigh him down ...
Paperback: 978-1-78279-936-8 ebook: 978-1-78279-937-5

The Cause
Roderick Vincent

The second American Revolution will be a fire lit from an internal spark.

Paperback: 978-1-78279-763-0 ebook: 978-1-78279-762-3

Don't Drink and Fly
The Story of Bernice O'Hanlon: Part One
Cathie Devitt

Bernice is a witch living in Glasgow. She loses her way in her life and wanders off the beaten track looking for the garden of enlightenment.

Paperback: 978-1-78279-016-7 ebook: 978-1-78279-015-0

Gag
Melissa Unger

One rainy afternoon in a Brooklyn diner, Peter Howland punctures an egg with his fork. Repulsed, Peter pushes the plate away and never eats again.

Paperback: 978-1-78279-564-3 ebook: 978-1-78279-563-6

The Master Yeshua
The Undiscovered Gospel of Joseph
Joyce Luck

Jesus is not who you think he is. The year is 75 CE. Joseph ben Jude is frail and ailing, but he has a prophecy to fulfil ...

Paperback: 978-1-78279-974-0 ebook: 978-1-78279-975-7

On the Far Side, There's a Boy
Paula Coston

Martine Haslett, a thirty-something 1980s woman, plays hard on the fringes of the London drag club scene until one night which prompts her to sign up to a charity. She writes to a young Sri Lankan boy, with consequences far and long.

Paperback: 978-1-78279-574-2 ebook: 978-1-78279-573-5

Tuareg
Alberto Vazquez-Figueroa
With over 5 million copies sold worldwide, Tuareg is a
classic adventure story from best-selling author Alberto Vazquez-
Figueroa, about honour, revenge and a clash of cultures.
Paperback: 978-1-84694-192-4

Readers of ebooks can buy or view any of these bestsellers by
clicking on the live link in the title. Most titles are published in
paperback and as an ebook. Paperbacks are available in traditional
bookshops. Both print and ebook formats are available online.

Find more titles and sign up to our readers' newsletter at
http://www.johnhuntpublishing.com/fiction

Follow us on Facebook at https://www.facebook.com/JHPfiction
and Twitter at https://twitter.com/JHPFiction